Mexico Sky

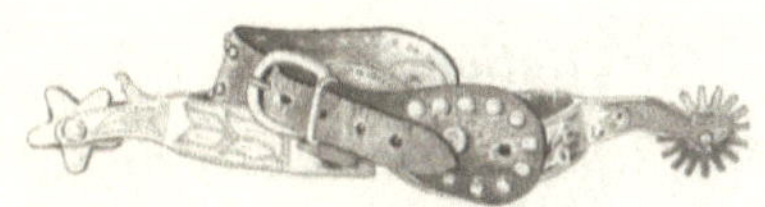

Look for other Western & Adventure
novels byEric H. Heisner

Along to Presidio

West to Bravo

Seven Fingers a' Brazos

Above the Llano

T. H. Elkman

Fire Angels

Short Western Tales: Friend of the Devil

Wings of the Pirate

Africa Tusk

Cicada

Citation for Murder

Conch Republic, Island Stepping with Hemingway

Conch Republic – vol. 2, Errol Flynn s Treasure

Conch Republic – vol. 3, Coba Libre

Follow book & film releases at:
www.leandogproductions.com

Mexico Sky

Eric H. Heisner

Illustration by Al P. Bringas

Visit our website at
www.leandogproductions.com

Illustration by: Al P. Bringas
Contact: al_bringas@yahoo.com

Cover design: Dreamscape Cover Designs
Edited by: Tim Haughian

Pocket Edition
Paperback ISBN: 978-956417-17-3

Dedication

To the strong-willed women …

Special Thanks

Ronald Heisner,
Amber Word Heisner & Al P. Bringas

Note from Author

Most of my stories revolve around the hardships and conflict of western men on the frontier. A lot of times the thing that drove those menfolk westward and the source behind their motivation to succeed was; women. Those hardy females had a variety of occupations that were accepted, but on the rare occurrence, some went beyond their social boundaries and did as they pleased in a world that catered to men.

Bandit queens such as Belle Starr, Etta Place and Pearl Hart were but a few that survived outside social norms. History is peppered with such stories and carried on through the strong females exemplified in the films of Howard Hawks, George Lucas and other storytellers. My father always said, "Behind every successful man – is a woman who demands it."

I hope you enjoy this western-adventure tale, from the turn of the previous century, which takes place as a wave of industrialization alters life at an ever-increasing pace.

Eric H. Heisner

September 9th, 2020

1

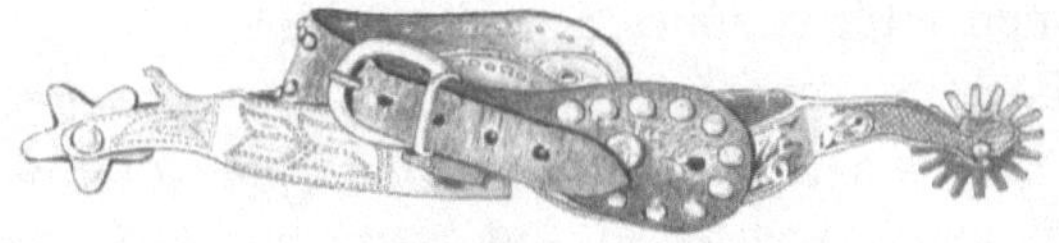

A haze of gunpowder smoke wafts down the main street. The largest building in town, the saloon, is under attack by a barrage of shots from across the way. With all sorts of rifles, shotguns and pistols, men take up positions behind barrels and water troughs. Constant pops of gunfire explode at random intervals as puffs of burnt discharge add to the fog-like blanket hanging over the center of the western town.

The front window pane shatters and rains glass down on a tipped-over table just inside the entryway to the saloon. Hunched down for cover behind the thick, wooden table top are two western-type figures with six-shooters ready in hand. The man on the left peeks over the shielding cover and stabs a shot from his pistol at one of the opposition across the street. The forty-five caliber lead thuds into the side of an empty barrel, and the man sheltered behind it hurries over to share cover with one of his compadres, behind a pile of mercantile supplies. Smoking firearm in hand, Pack Stevens is outfitted like a Montana cowboy with his wide-brimmed hat, colorful bandana, waist-sash and pants tucked in to tall-leather boots. From a freshly-shaven face, his ever-ready smile flashes to his partner squatted down at his side behind the upturned table. "Damn, where did all these fellas come from?"

Head bowed down while ejecting empty brass casings from a gun, Elliott Wayne aims a reprimanding gaze at Pack. "The next time I say let's go to Mexico, we go to Mexico..."

Aiming his revolver over the top of the table again, Pack lets off another pistol shot. A fusillade of fired bullets returns in reply, as splinters of wood leap from the edge of the tabletop, and the glass globe of a lamp smashes to the floor. Pack looks innocently over at Elliott and shakes his head. "Yeah, next time..."

Finished with reloading the handgun, Elliott pokes the gun barrel over the tabletop and hammers off another shot. Dressed in much the same fashion as Pack, with medium-cropped hair, the twosome appears to be a couple of old-time western cowboys. Elliott glimpses at Pack and grumbles, "That's what you said last time."

Shooting his pistol at random targets across the street, Pack hunkers down again and ejects the six spent brass shells. He looks down to his own nearly-empty ammunition belt and then over to Elliott. He reaches over to pluck a cartridge from his partner's waist and counts the remainder. "Is that it?

Aiming a pistol over the table, Elliott grimaces. "There's more on the horses."

Selecting the target carefully, Elliott's firearm barks, and Pack watches a man with a bullet-crease across his buttocks jump up from behind a hitching post. He tilts his head and reprimands his partner with a glare, "Easy pard, you could've killed him."

Elliott smirks and replies, "Not with a shot to the ass, 'nless his head is stuck up there."

Pack finishes reloading his pistol, six around, and peeks over the barroom table. "We need to get clear of here."

Elliott looks at their supply of ammunition and sighs. "It's no good pulling these types of cons anymore, when we get about twenty dollars in coin and have to shoot our way out with forty dollars' worth of lead."

Pack ducks down lower as another volley of gunfire from the street smashes through the saloon. "We got twenty-five last time and didn't have to shoot our way out!"

Staying down low, away from the barrage of gunshots, Elliott carefully peeks around the side of the turned over table. Bullets bounce across the floorboards, and the sound of a ricochet is followed by another smash of breaking glass. Elliott pulls back and looks at Pack. Squinting at him in a supportive, yet critical manner, they exchange a look. "It's just a bad con, that's all. We near got tarred 'n feathered in Virginia City."

"Well, we ain't no bank robbers, rustlers or gamblers. Pulling a good hoodwink never lost me any sleep at night."

"That's what I'm saying. It ain't a good hoodwink."

Pack looks at his partner and puts on a charming grin. "Jest needs practice, is all."

Befuddled, Elliott takes off her hat, shakes out her hair and is revealed to be a rather attractive-looking female. She glares at Pack and then winces, as several more rounds of projectiles smack into the tabletop hiding them. "If we ever get clear of here and keep pulling that old one, all we're gonna get is more shootin' practice."

"That's fine. Next meal is on you."

As Elliott gives her partner a sweet, sarcastic smile, she is interrupted by a booming explosion coming from the street. The blast rattles the peeling paint from every wood-framed storefront in town. They exchange looks of astonishment, then both peek out from the cover of the table. Elliott smiles brightly and exclaims, "Hot-damn, there's Griz!"

With a wide grin, Pack gives his pistol a twirling spin on his forefinger. "And he's a comin' on fast!"

2

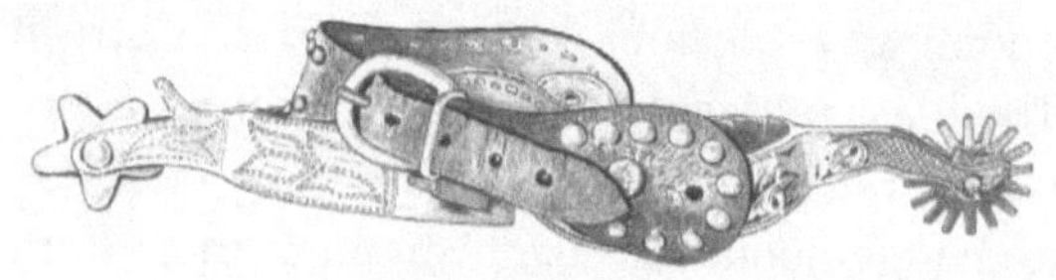

A four-wheeled supply wagon, pulled by a dual horse rig trailing two saddled mounts races down the wide, dirt street. Sitting atop the driver's bench seat, a grizzled old man slaps a set of leather lead lines across the rumps of the horse team. The tough-as-nails, eccentric personality, Griz, chomps a lit cigar in his teeth and holds several sticks of dynamite clenched under his arm. He lights a dangling fuse and hollers, "Kick up some dust 'nd make like a jackrabbit a-fire!"

Griz tosses the stick of dynamite with the smoking fuse just in time for it to explode at the front porch of the building directly across from the saloon. As men scramble away, the horse team shies from the exploding blast and debris showers down over the town. The old-timer driving the wagon gives a shrill whistle and tries to slow the horse team's running pace. The saddle horses trailing behind the wagon kick and buck in protest. "Whoa there, ya jack-a-napes… I say whoa!"

From inside the saloon, Pack and Elliott watch in utter amazement. With guns in hand, they simultaneously vault over the bullet-riddled tabletop and dash out into the street. The smoke from the big explosion swirls aside as Griz steers the wagon past the saloon and slows the team to a canter. "C'mon, you two! Let's skedaddle!" As Elliott leaps from the boardwalk, followed closely by her saddle partner, the batwing doors at the front of the saloon slap together and swing freely in opposing directions. Grabbing just behind the front wheel, she takes a hold of the wagon bed's low sidewall. Pack grabs her waist and boosts her up and inside behind the driver's bench seat. Griz glimpses over his shoulder and snorts, as he lights another stick of dynamite with his cigar. "Glad to have ya back again, Missy."

Tripping over his large-roweled spurs, Pack falls, misses his grasp at the wagon and nearly gets rolled over by the rear wheel and trampled by the trailing pair of horses. Elliott sits upright in the back of the wagon, just as Griz tosses the other stick of dynamite into a smoking arc through the air. The explosion rocks the boardwalk, as armed men scramble for cover. Elliott looks back to see Pack, alone in the street, following after them in a full-out run. "Griz! Stop the wagon!"

Cigar still clenched in his teeth, Griz glimpses over his shoulder, as he tugs at the horse team's lead lines to no effect. "Sorry Missy, the dyno got 'em spooked. Have to run 'er out."

Elliott watches, as Pack continues to follow their dusty back-trail and several angry, armed townsmen take up the foot chase. She waves her arm, urging him to run faster. "Hurry, Pack."

Hauling-ass down the street after the fleeing wagon, Pack returns shots haphazardly over his shoulder toward the mob. In return, several indiscriminate gunshots whiz over his head while others skitter off the dirt street around his feet. Finally, his pistol clicks on an empty chamber. He looks behind at the angry pursuers before quickening his pace. "Hold up there, Griz! Elliott...!"

Drawing her belt knife from the sheath, Elliott swipes at the lead rope to one of the saddle horses and cuts it free. She watches as the separated horse keeps pace next to the other for a short while then lingers back and slows to a trot.

Behind the speeding wagon, Pack holsters his spent sidearm and kicks up some dust while trying not to trip on his spurs again. As the untethered horse slows, Pack runs up behind and vaults into the empty saddle. He takes hold of the loose reins, grips his legs firmly and jabs his spurred heels to the animal's flank. The startled mount rears up, spins around, then charges ahead after the wagon.

Still being pursued by the ill-tempered, gun-firing mob, Pack urges the racing steed onward, as gunshots zip past him. In a goodbye gesture, he lifts a hand skyward and rides on. Just beyond the town buildings, the shooting finally ceases. The steady cadence of the running footfalls fade into the distance, as the wagon and lone rider disappear from sight.

~*~

In a remote section of woods, several hours from town, a small campfire casts light around the circle of companions. The horses are tethered nearby, and the wagon stands unhitched. Griz hobbles over to the campfire, as Elliott speaks across the jumping flames to Pack, seated on the ground. "Down Mexico way is where we should be heading."

Griz hocks the collected results of a hacking cough aside and wipes the lingering spittle from his beard whiskers. "It's kinder nice down there. Folks are real poor, but ya don't need much to get by."

Tilting his head in disagreement, Pack turns a wary eye up at Griz and then back across the fire to his female partner. "Why not California?"

Elliott fakes a shiver, pulling her coat close at her neck, "It's cold in California."

Expressions illuminated by the campfire, the two men exchange a mystified look and Pack responds sardonically, "Only to you it is. Most the time it is like no weather at all."

"Well, the beaches are cold anyway."

From across the campfire, Pack grimaces and states. "Hell, Elliott, I ain't much of a swimmer."

"In Mexico you would be. The nights are plenty warm, the beer is cold and the ocean salt water is like a warm bath."

Griz sniffs and shrugs. "I ain't much on baths."

They both look to the older man in his dirty, tattered wardrobe and Elliott remarks. "Nor on doing laundry."

Pack lies back on the ground, using his saddle-seat as a pillow, and tips his hat over his eyes. "We ever get enough dust to last us a bit, maybe we'll head to Mexico."

Elliott shakes her head incredulously, while Griz squats on his haunches, coughs, and then mutters over toward Pack. "You two young'uns gonna stick with that same old con job and shoot yer way down there?"

Pack lifts the wide brim of his hat slightly and casts a glaring look at Griz. His gaze travels over to Elliott, as she snickers with amusement. Pack lets down his hat and grunts, "I'll think of something. Don't you two worry 'bout it none." He shifts to his side, pulling his blanket over his shoulder.

Elliott lies back on her saddle gear and makeshift pallet of blankets then stares up at the starry sky. "I'll stick with ya Pack, same as always."

Griz grunts, as he finds a comfy spot next to the fire. "Me too. I'll stick."

Elliott continues to stare skyward, while the orange firelight flickers a warm glow on her high cheekbones and feminine features. "Boys, that Mexico sky may not have all the bright stars like Montana, but at least it's still free."

3

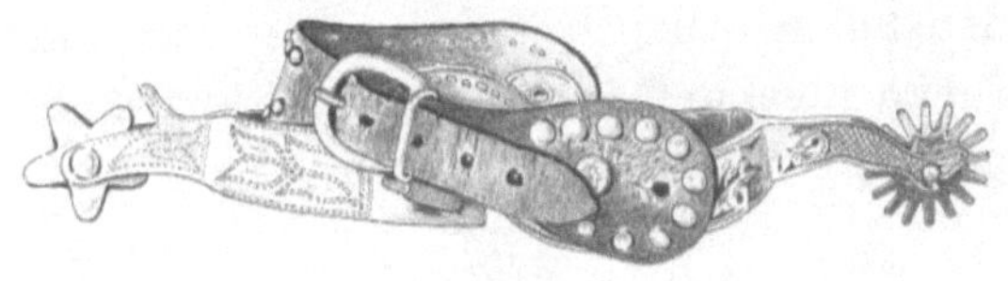

Pack and Elliott ride into another western town, followed by Griz in the supply wagon. They dismount their horses in front of a general store and scan the moderately-sized boomtown. The wagon stops in the street, and Pack turns back to Griz. "Hey pard, how about you replenish our food supplies here. Elliott and I will have a look-see at our prospects."

Pack takes a few coins out from his vest pocket and tosses them to Griz. He turns to Elliott, as she gazes around to study the lay of the town. "What do ya think?"

She ties her horse next to his and shrugs her shoulders. "Saloon is always a good start."

Griz heartily replies, "That's my perspective on life." The old-timer climbs down from the wagon, shakes his head, laughs and jingles the coins in his palm. "I'll be in there shortly to join ya for a drink." He steps to the boardwalk and watches, as Pack and Elliott make their way across the mud-rutted street to the largest of the drinking and gaming establishments in town.

~*~

The interior of the saloon is filled with cowboys, gamblers and miners, along with every other multifarious western personality. Standing at the bar, two men sip from tumblers of whiskey while they scan the occupants of the crowded watering hole. The apparent leader of the pair, Hank, wears a shiny, nickel-plated revolver high on his hip and has the sharp, exacting eye of a fox in a hen house.

His associate, Fisk, follows his partner's every move, ready to back him up in whatever sort of deed that may arise. It doesn't escape the observation of the drinking duo when Pack follows Elliott through the saloon's bat-wing doors. Hank murmurs over to Fisk, "Huh! I'll be... Lookee there."

Elliott pulls her hat low on her forehead in an attempt to hide her feminine features, as Pack moves around past her. He proceeds to the length of bar and waves at the bartender busy at the other end of the room. At the sound of a familiar grunting voice, he turns his attention.

"Well, Pack Stevens. What brings you this far south? They must've already run you out of every sportin' town and gaming hall in the northern frontier."

Pack pivots around to face Hank. "Hello there, Hank." He merely glances at Fisk and nods half-heartedly. "Fisk."

Hank reaches out his open hand and gives Pack an excessively friendly shake, while he grins devilishly at Elliott. "Got yerself a partner, eh?"

Pack gestures to Elliott, as she adjusts her brim up a bit. "Fellas, this is Miss Wayne."

Hank gives a crafty wink and extends his hand to her. "Yes… I know Miss Wayne."

Pack seems surprised. "You do?"

Hank raises Elliott's hand up to his lips and gives it a kiss. "How the hell are you, Elliott? After we quit each other some time back, I figured you'd stoop to a better class of character than this."

Annoyed, she pulls her hand away from Hank's lips, and her eyes flit toward Pack. "I did."

Pack listens to their acquainted banter with a twinge of jealousy, until Hank turns his attention back to him and asks, "What ya drinking there, Packey?"

"Beer."

Hank smiles knowingly. "Working, huh?"

Elliott steps to the bar, nudging her way between them. "I'll have the same."

Hank raises his eyebrows at her, and subtly smirks. "Nothing stronger, perhaps? How about I get ya your usual?" Before she can utter a reply, Hank looks at Pack and lifts his glass of whiskey from the bar top. "No need to waste yer time on one of them silly tricks you pull." He takes a short sip. "Fisk 'nd I have a job in the makin' that could use two more." He pokes his elbow out to jab Elliott in the ribs and continues, "A lady would fit the bill just perfect."

Elliott stares hard at Hank. "What about Griz?"

Surprised, Hank puts his drink of whiskey down and turns to Pack. "Griz? Is he still alive yet? Gol-damn, he must be a hundred years old by now. Hell, he's in too, if he wants."

Fisk takes a sip from his own whiskey and grumbles. "Ain't splittin' my share with some old decrepit hanger-on."

Pack leans over the bar, and tries to get the bartender's attention again while Elliott looks over and smiles insincerely at Fisk. She murmurs. "We ain't interested anyhow."

Hank positions himself right between Elliott and Fisk. "Don't worry about it honey, Griz is in."

Fisk thumps his glass and speaks, "I said…"

Hank sternly glares back over his shoulder at Fisk, as he stomps his boot heel onto his partner's toe. "Easy pard… You work with who I say."

Fisk yelps and pulls his boot back to hop on one foot. "For cripes-sake Hank!"

"Understood?"

"Yeah pard."

Glancing aside from his leaned over position on the bar slab, Pack adds, "Like the lady said, we ain't interested."

Hank keeps it friendly. "Now, hear me out."

Elliott shakes her head, as Pack receives two beers slid down the bar-top. "We don't want anything to do with it."

Turning, Pack hands off one of the fresh glasses of beer to Elliott. Fisk gripes under his breath, as Hank continues with a grin, "Listen to what I have to say, and then we'll leave you be." As Pack and Elliott stand, frothing beverages in hand, both turn their attention to Hank as he leans in closer to talk.

~*~

The clamor inside the saloon increases as patrons filter in and the day progresses. Hank buys each of them another round and continues in his attempt to entice their partnership. Elliott finally excuses herself from the group. She makes her way to the gold-painted sign at the rear of the saloon which reads, in scrawled letters, *Shitters – out back.*

Stepping outside from the back door of the building, Elliott descends several sets of stairs and crosses the alleyway to a lineup of four side-by-side, wood-framed outhouses. Hiking up her gun belt and holster, she unfastens her britches. She swings the door open to the first privy and steps inside.

4

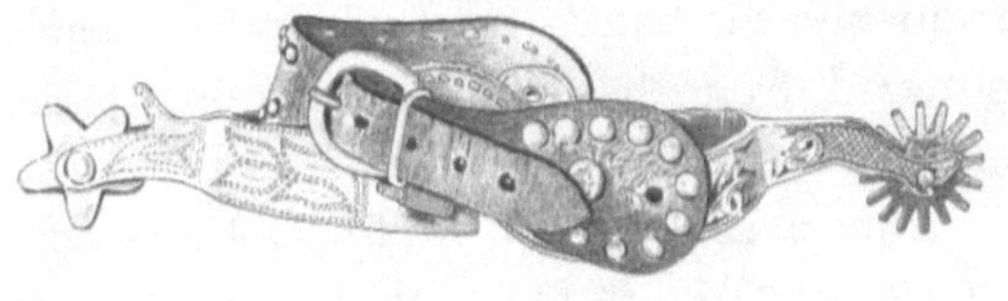

Down the street from the main saloon, a lone horseman loiters in the street along with several other saddled horses. An explosion of gunshots comes from inside the bank, and puffs of spent gun-powder billow out from the opened door. A guard rushes outside, pulls the door closed behind him and slides his watchman's club through the handle. Another popping snap of gunshots splinters the door from inside, and the guard spins to the boardwalk, wounded, and yells, "Holdup!"

At the sound of the verbal alarm, armed pedestrians, along with a few badge-wearing lawmen, swarm the street. The sound of a shotgun thunders and the rider with the getaway horses is blasted out of his saddle. The bank robber's untethered mounts scatter in every direction, as the crowd in the street assembles around the brick building. Suddenly, the bank's front window explodes outward, from the impact of a thrown table, and is followed by another series of gunshots.

Almost simultaneously, five robbers leap from the broken frame of glass with a canvas money sack in one hand and a blazing pistol in the other. Citizens duck for cover and return fire. Scattering along the front walkway, the thieves dodge bullets from the vigilante townsfolk, as they seek any means of escape.

One of the bank robbers dashes after a loose horse by the boardwalk and is aggressively shot at by multiple citizens. Seeing their cohort mercilessly gunned-down in the street, two of the holdup men duck into a barber shop next door to the bank and return gunfire from the doorway and windows. As the attempted escape quickly deteriorates from bad to worse, the remaining two bandits duck into a narrow alley. Guns blazing, they make their way to the rear of the building.

~*~

From a second story hotel window, far across the street, a man obscured by shadow observes the commotion in the street. He turns to speak with someone else in the room, then faces back to the window and draws the curtains partly shut. In shaded profile, the mysterious gentleman continues to watch the foiled robbery unfold, as shouting voices of townspeople gradually replace the popping echo of gunfire.

~*~

Inside the wooden shell of the outdoor toilet, Elliott sits in relative privacy, with her pants gathered around her ankles. She hears the distant popping sound of gunshots coming from the main street and quickly finishes her task. Standing to pull up and fasten her britches, she hears some men hurriedly approaching.

They stop in front of the lineup of latrines and one of them yanks at the door, finding it secured from the inside. "Someone in there?" The man violently pulls at the door handle in an attempt to bust the locking latch.

With a bang, the flimsy door to the next outhouse swings open, and the other robber speaks in gasping breaths. "Here... Put 'em both in this one."

"Are you kidding?"

"I'd rather launder it later than hang for it now."

"Aww, shit!"

"Exactly..."

After the sound of two consecutive splashes, the wood door slams shut. Grumbling, the two outlaws dash away and out of earshot. Muted voices from afar cry out, as the gunfire ceases. The wailing sound of a wounded horse is heard, followed by a silencing gunshot.

Inside the first stall, a dismayed Elliott stands frozen, clutching her britches up around her waist. She undoes the door latch and peeks out into the alley behind the saloon. With a creak and bang of the latrine door, Elliott steps out with her pants unfastened and her holster-belt slung loosely over her hips.

5

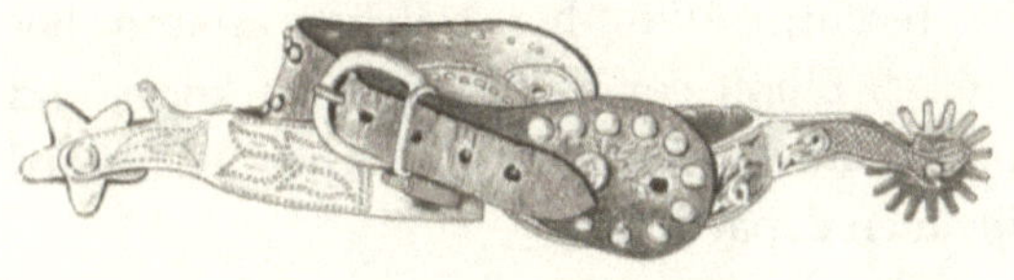

An armed crowd of townspeople makes their way down the alleyway, searching every backdoor, crevice and hiding spot. They reach the assemblage of outdoor toilets and swing open the first door to find it empty. One of the men leans in to peer down the dark, gaping hole and pulls back, repulsed by the overwhelming odor of urine and feces.

The second door handle is tried, only to find it locked. The armed men gather around, all aiming their weapons, and then forcefully yank open the outhouse door to reveal Elliott seated on the toilet box. Covering herself, embarrassed, she brushes her hair away from her forehead and forces a smile. "Excuse me, gentlemen…"

One of the lawmen steps forward, lowers his double-barreled shotgun and tips his hat to her. "I'm sorry, ma'am." Aware of her compromised position, he blocks the crowd of peepers behind him as he questions her. "Bank was robbed. Did you hear anyone pass by recent?" With her britches around her ankles, Elliott covers her exposed knees and points off down the alley to where she heard the men depart.

"Thank you, ma'am."

The law officer nods kindly and apologetically closes the stall door, leaving Elliott to her business.

~*~

The interior of the saloon is hushed with the murmuring of several patrons discussing the commotion down the street. Pack, standing at the bar with Hank and Fisk, starts to grow concerned about his partner's overdue return. Hank notices Pack repeatedly glancing to the rear exit door where they last saw her leave. "Ya never know about women… Maybe she got sensible and took off with those bank robbers. The three of us can make this little job work without her." Hank gets a reticent look from Pack and adds, "Griz too, of course."

Pack can't help but return his gaze to the back door as he replies to Hank, "She'll be back soon enough, I think. Neither of us is interested in going to jail."

Hank shrugs, and takes a drink. "Who is?"

Standing alongside, Fisk sips his own whiskey and shakes his head. "Forget about that pants-wearin' woman." He lowers the tumbler and snorts aside to Hank and Pack. "She'll come 'round when you have lots of money to spend. All the one's I know don't stick when you ain't got no dust. Let's do this thing without her."

Pack glares at Fisk and then returns his attention to Hank. "Me and Elliott are headin' south. We ain't interested."

Smoothing his index finger around the rim of his glass, Hank tilts his head over toward Pack and murmurs low, "Things sure ain't any easier in Texas. They're so sick of con-men and outlaws, they shoot first and don't worry 'bout who you are till they mark out a gravestone."

Fisk leans over and pipes in, "Hell, you know what they did to ol' John Wesley in El Paso…"

Pack takes a sip from his beer. "He was a gunfighter and a pain in the ass. Besides, that was quite a few years past. This is a new century and things change."

"The fun is all gone out West." Hank shakes his head remorsefully and continues. "It ain't like it was ten years ago. Now it's full of women and children who want a daddy who will work in the town store and sit down at the table for the evenin' meal. We got to get our take while the gettin's good. Those payroll robbers had the right idea… It's just that they did it with guns instead of brains."

Fisk finishes his drink and thumps his glass on the bar. "C'mon Hank, let's find someone else. He's too worried about the woman to be of any use to us. I say, he's a step out of the grave and headin' for a town job."

Pack frowns at Fisk and pulls Hank aside to talk alone. "I just want to go over it all with Elliott first and consider it." He hooks his thumb over his shoulder at Fisk and grunts, "She's a helluva better hand in a jam than that one."

Hank slaps his hand on Pack's shoulder and smirks. "Let me talk with her. We got history, us two."

Suddenly the barroom doors burst open and a badge-wearing deputy rushes in and pulls up a chair to stand on. The saloon occupants all turn their attention, as he peers out over the anticipating crowd. "As you folks have heard, the bank was broke into not more'n thirty minutes ago. Most of the cash has been recovered, along with the guilty culprits." The deputy raises his shotgun across his chest and continues to address the assembly. "Two of them have absconded with a cut of the hold-up in the amount of twenty-thousand dollars."

The room becomes abuzz with excitement at the mention of the amount of stolen money. The deputy holds up his hands for quiet and speaks louder. "There has been a reward put up for the recovery of the remaining thieves." Pointing the barrel of his shotgun out the front doors for emphasis, the deputy scans the attentive faces before him. "We are organizing a posse in front of the sheriff's station. You have to supply your own horse, saddle tack and guns. We'll be supplying the ammunition."

Fisk leans an elbow behind on the bar top and hollers, "If twenty grand is the prize, then how much is the reward?"

The deputy stays atop the chair and speaks out to the unruly crowd. "One hundred dollars will be awarded to the men who recover the stolen money and help to apprehend criminals."

Fisk snorts aside to Hank, "I ain't turnin' twenty grand in for a split on no hundred bucks."

The deputy steps down from his high perch and waves an arm for anyone to follow, as he moves to the front door. Hank moves alongside Pack and speaks quietly to him while they watch the deputy lead some of the bar patrons outside. "See what I mean, Packey? The fun is all over 'round here." Moving his leg to the side, Hank taps Fisk's boot heel as a signal, then finishes his drink and sets it down on the bar-top. He shakes his head at Pack. "Forget about talking to Elliott. We can do it another time." He nods at Fisk toward the exit. "See ya around, Pack."

Fisk heads for the swinging saloon doors. Hank smiles a curious grin while leaving the bar to follow him outside. Pack leans back on the bar-slab to look around the mostly quieted saloon. As he takes a swig of his nearly empty mug of beer, he sniffs the air and smells something extremely foul. Pack turns to see Elliott approaching from behind him and notices her boots and pants are smeared with some sort of wet, greasy mud all the way up to her thigh. "What happened to you?" He gives another inquisitive sniff and looks at her queerly. "You fall in?"

She nods to the back entrance door. "Let's get out of here."

Pack sniffs again curiously. "Shit, is that you?!?"

"Yeah… Come out back." Elliott moves toward the rear exit. Pack takes another swallow of his beer, rubs his nose to stifle the smell, and then he follows her outside.

6

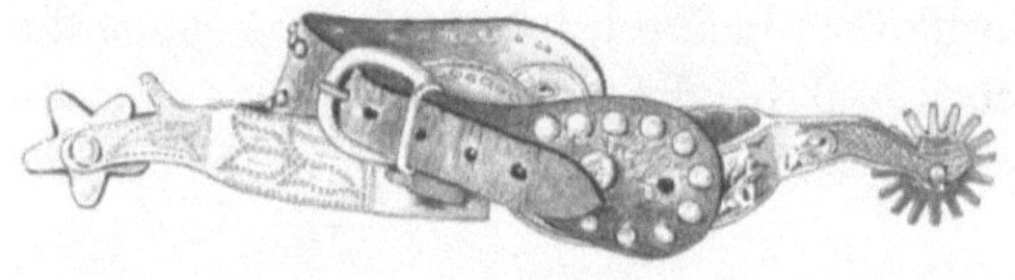

Walking the crowded boardwalk, following Elliott, Pack weaves through the townsfolk still milling around after the robbery. Startled, people wince in disgust at the strong odor coming from Elliott's trousers. As he speaks to her, Pack tries not to inhale too deeply. "What's going on with you?"

She continues to make her way through the throngs of citizens lingering in the street, until she reaches their wagon. As Griz loads food and supplies, Elliott climbs onto her saddle-mount without saying a word to either of them and steers into the busy street. Grabbing her horse by the halter, Pack steps alongside Elliott and the offensive scent from her pants is almost too much to bear. "I don't know what you did, but we need to get you some new trousers."

"Griz got some for me. Throw a leg over and let's go already."

Pack looks down the main road and sees Hank, Fisk and others assembling for the posse. "Where are we going? There's decent money could be made in this town if we stay." He looks to Griz for support as the old-timer climbs onto the wagon seat, but only receives a shrug in reply. When Pack lets go of Elliott's horse, she gather the reins between her fingers and starts to ride away. Pack looks after her and grumbles. "Gol' dammit. Who's running this outfit?"

Griz flashes a toothy grin, as he spits tobacco juice beside the wheel. "Let's foller along 'n find out?"

Pack's shoulders droop, as he watches his partner trot off. "Shit..." Stepping over to his horse, Pack leaps on and spins the animal to point in Elliott's direction.

~*~

Halfway through town, Pack rides up alongside Elliott and glances over his shoulder to the congregation of newly-appointed deputies being sworn-in at the Sheriff's office.

"That posse is headed out of town in the other direction."

Without looking back, Elliott responds, "Good."

Frustrated, Pack shakes his head and looks to see Griz coming along behind in the wagon. "You know, Elliott, this is why I don't play poker with you..."

She merely smiles to herself and continues to ride southward, out of town, followed by Pack and Griz.

~*~

The gentleman in the upper hotel window studies the street as he lights a fresh cigar, held between pinched fingers. He puts the rolled-wand of tobacco to his lips and steadily puffs until the end begins to glow. Through the wavy glass window pane, he watches as a posse of horsemen is assembled among the crowd of townspeople.

His gaze shifts to the far end of town as two riders travel south, followed by an older man in a supply wagon. Turning to address the room, the gentleman blows out a cloud of smoke and looks at the individuals awaiting their orders. "Gather some men for the posse. We have a trail to follow." The hired men all nod in unison and turn to exit the room.

7

Several miles outside town, on a secluded section of the road, Elliott turns her mount around and rides over to the wagon. Flashing a perceptive grin beneath his grey, bristly whiskers, Griz tosses her a brand new pair of pants. She tucks the folded trousers under one arm and steers her horse away from the path toward a nearby stand of trees. Pack watches her move off the trail and turns to Griz. "Where's she going?"

The old-timer merely spits a long stream of tobacco and gives another whiskered grin. "You know better'n to ask why a woman do what she do."

Giving his horse a kick, Pack steers away from the road and lopes his horse toward the concealing patch of woods. Pack's gelding maneuvers his way through the trees and snorts with recognition, as they approach Elliott's steed. Having just disrobed below the waist, she smiles playfully and looks up to Pack from under the neck of her horse. "Figured you'd get yerself a peep?"

Embarrassed, Pack coughs to clear his throat and turns his stare from her shapely, feminine legs. "I jest want to know what the hell has gotten into you of late." His curious gaze darts to her exposed lower half again, before he turns his horse away and continues. "Ever since you saw that damned Hank in town, you've been actin' weird."

Elliott grabs the pair of clean britches from over the saddle, and lifts up her leg to pull them on. She hops on one foot and works one leg into the clean trousers. Half-dressed, Elliott peeks over the saddle to her partner and answers, "How do you mean... acting weird?"

Pack glimpses over to see a portion of her naked thigh and quickly looks away again. "I hardly know what to think. We barely say two words to each other in the saloon, then we up and leave a perfectly good town that was ripe for action." Pack gazes out to the road where Griz has traveled a short distance ahead with the wagon, then sighs, "Don't be dropping hints... Should we be heading our separate ways?"

Now filly dressed, Elliott steps out from behind her horse and looks up at Pack. "Now Pack, I've never been one to complain or throw hints, and I've always told you straight." She looks down as she does up the button fly on her britches and then at the road to where the wagon has gone on ahead. "Let's get a little further away from town before I tell you." Shaking out her tall leather boots, she pulls them on, despite their dampness, and crinkles her nose at the offensive smell.

Pack catches a telling whiff and looks down to her britches in the grass. "What did you get into?"

Elliott shrugs and chuckles. "I've stepped in worse." She swings up into the saddle and turns her mount toward the path traveled by Griz and the wagon. Looking over her shoulder, she gives Pack a sultry grin. "Mister Pack Stevens, you do look a mite bit out of sorts. I hope it wasn't jealousy of that ol' Hank that put the green in your complexion..."

Pack snuffles his nose and tries to clear it of the stench. "I wanted to talk to you about him while we were in town."

She gives her mount a kick with her heels and trots off. "Yes... We'll talk about it later." Not seeming to have a choice in the timing of the discussion, Pack takes a deep breath. Befuddled, he glances at the heap of soiled britches left behind and shakes his head. Adjusting his hat, he follows after her.

~*~

Twelve men on horseback canter down the road, led by the mysterious gentleman from the hotel window. At a cluster of tracks in the roadway, the group halts at the signal of the half-breed Indian scout dressed in a fringed buckskin outfit. The scout studies the dusty trail and dismounts to take a closer look. He gestures fingers toward the woods and remarks, "Two split off here."

The horses snort and blow for air while the horsemen look for any signs of activity in the nearby stand of trees. Proceeding on foot, the half-breed leads his horse away from the main road and follows the fresh set of tracks. As the posse follows, the scout leads through the trees to find a wadded-up bundle of clothing on the ground. He gives the dark-colored pile an inquisitive kick and winces at the foul odor it emits. "Hmm… Smells of shit!"

Positioned at the head of the posse, the gentleman rides forward and looks down at the discarded item on the ground. "What is that?" The scout looks up at the man and shrugs. "Them smell of soiled britches."

The mysterious gentleman takes a fresh cigar from his coat pocket and licks the uncut end of the tobacco. In thought, he looks over to his right-hand man and nods his head. "Stokes, pick them up and bring them along."

The horseback man directly beside the gentleman catches the foul odor and calls down to the Indian tracker. "You heard what he said. Pick 'em up."

Everyone looks down at the half-breed, as he shakes his head disagreeably. "No, sir. I won't."

Stokes leans an elbow on his saddle horn and watches, as the scout pokes the smeared trousers with a long stick. Shaking his head, he grimaces. "Don't know what that's about, but they can't be far ahead." He looks up to the late day sun and calculates the time. "We can camp for the night and find 'em tomorrow."

The leader of the posse spits the chewed-off end from the cigar and strikes a match on the leg of his pants. He puts the flame to the tip of the tobacco and his gaze travels around. As a puff of smoke escapes from his lips, he gestures with a nod to the edge of the clustered trees. "We'll camp there." Nudging his sweated horse forward, the smoking gentleman rides casually to the clearing.

As the horsemen dismount to make camp, two of the riders travel back to the main road. They gaze down the empty path and exchange a knowing glance before deciding to return to the campsite with the other posse members. The riders begin to unsaddle and Fisk speaks to Hank, "Never can trust where a woman will lead."

8

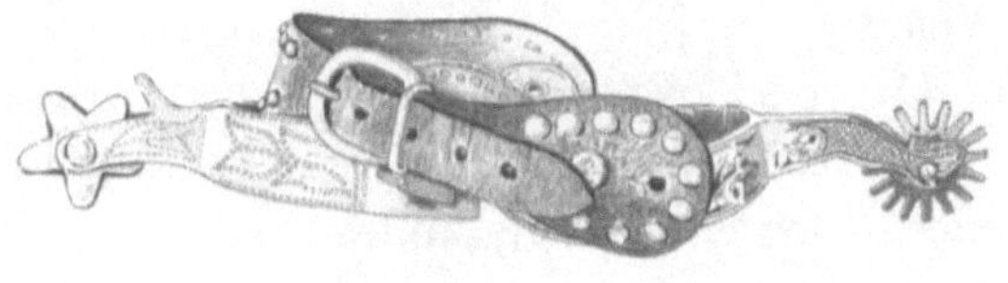

A small campfire lights up the dark night, and the familiar evening call of a great horned owl echoes in the cool breeze. Cast iron clanks while Griz cleans the pot from their supper. Pack sits across from Elliott, impatiently watching her through the glowing flames as she finishes her meal. Wiping her chin, she looks at him. "Is something wrong, Pack?"

"Yes."

"What is it?"

"You tell me."

She puts her dish aside and gets up. Griz takes their plates and wipes them with a grungy-looking wash towel. Pack watches, as she goes to the wagon and pulls out two muddy-looking cloth sacks from under the supplies in the back of the bed. She carries them to Pack, tosses them at his feet and shrugs innocently.

Confused, Pack looks down at the canvas sacks and catches the familiar, awful scent. "Okay… They stink to high-heaven, too. What's inside?"

"Have a look."

Wincing at the odor, Pack pulls one of the bags closer. He gingerly unties the drawstring and peers into the opening. Puzzled, he briefly looks up to Elliott before reaching his hand inside and feeling around. "Where is this from?"

Elliott's eyes light up with excitement. "That appears to be two-fifths of that hold-up money."

Looking down and pulling out a handful of currency, Pack stares at it in amazement. "Where did you get it?"

"In the crapper."

"No shit?"

She laughs, and crinkles her nose. "Well, a little."

Not believing his eyes, Pack turns his attention over to Griz. "You know about this, old man?"

The old-timer merely shrugs and leans on the wagon. "Figured she'd have a good reason for stinkin' like she was 'n gittin' gone in a hurry."

Disregarding the stench, Pack reaches into the sack and shuffles his hand around to get a rough estimate of the cash. Still shocked, he looks up at Elliott "How much is here?"

"I don't know."

Griz coughs and spits alongside the wagon's wheel. "Question is: What're ye gonna do with it?"

As Elliott stares down at Pack with the open money bag before him, he glances up to meet her questioning expression. She nudges the other robbery sack toward him and grins. "Yeah, partner... What are we going to do with it?"

~*~

The morning air has a chill to it, as Griz drives the wagon along the mountain road at a slow, leisurely pace. Suddenly, the posse of twelve horsemen thunders down the narrow path and quickly surrounds the wagon. To the sounds of agitated horses stomping and the loud clicking of firearms, Griz eases back on the reins and scans the faces in the crowd.

At the front of the group, alongside the gentleman leader, Stokes turns toward the wagon. "Hold up there, you!" The horse team rears up and Griz pulls the slack reins. Wheeling his horse around to face the wagon, Stokes aims a cocked pistol at Griz and calls out, "Throw down yer arms."

Surrounded, Griz acquiesces to the request of the horseback men. He slowly reaches down behind his feet and then throws out a double-barreled shotgun. Stokes sidesteps his mount closer to the wagon and peers down toward the man's boots. "Is that it?"

Griz takes the stub of chewed cigar from between his teeth and spits between the legs of the closest man's horse. "That's the one to be 'feared of since it's the one I kin reach." The horsemen begin to settle, and Griz actively chews on the damp end of his unlit cigar while he studies the firearms pointed his way. Noticing one of the posse members is dressed better than the others, he directs his questions to him. "You in charge here? What's this about?"

The mysterious gentleman eyes the whiskered old man and takes a cigar from his coat pocket. "You know who I am?"

Griz shifts his cigar to the side of his mouth and grunts in response. "Nope, but I figured I'd talk with you since you're the only one not pointing a gun at me."

The horseback leader nods, as he lights his cigar and then gestures to the riders. "Search the wagon."

Two of the riders climb down from their horses and start to shift through the piled contents of the wagon bed. Eventually, everyone lowers the aim of their firearms after nothing is found. Blowing out a puff of smoke in rings, the leader of the posse studies Griz intently, and the old man asks, "Ya got another of them expensive tobacco smokes fer me?" The old-timer takes the chewed cigar stub from his mouth and examines the mashed-flat, wet tip.

The lead horseman shakes his head curtly and replies, "Where are your riding companions?"

Scratching under his beard, Griz sits back against the driver's bench backrest and shrugs. "They're gone."

"Where have they gone?"

"You know how flighty them young people today are. Always going this way 'n that, never telling you what they's up to, or why. Just this mornin', I woke up by my lonesome, so I figured I'd head up into the hills for a little prospecting."

"Prospecting?"

The old-timer chuckles gleefully. "For gold, that is... I'm too old to be searching after women."

The horseback leader sits up straighter and deliberately takes a drag from his cigar. "When are they coming back?"

Griz appears to be puzzled. "Comin' back to where? They ain't goin' nowhere's that I'm headed, far as I know."

Stokes moves his mount alongside the posse leader and holsters his sidearm. He looks to the trail ahead and then back in the direction from where they came. "They might have doubled back, or could be further up the trail."

Tossing his partly smoked cigar aside, the mysterious gentleman turns to evaluate the assembly of posse members. He gestures toward two men at the back of the group, and utters a command, "You two there! Take him back to town and hold him until our return."

Everyone is quiet, as Hank looks aside to Fisk, peers around and realizes that the command was directed at them. "Uh, we'd rather not." They duck their heads away, as Griz peers over his shoulder in their direction.

Stokes barks, "You'll do as you're told, understand?" The second-in-command turns his horse and glares at them.

Fisk keeps his eyes averted, as Hank smiles graciously and replies, "Sure… No problem. We'll get 'im back to town."

Stokes looks at the leader of the posse, who confirms with a nod. Grimly, Stokes pushes his horse by Hank and Fisk and speaks to them over his shoulder, "Don't let him or that wagon out of your sight, ya hear?" Stokes continues down the trail following after the gentleman, as the others fall in behind.

Griz watches as the posse, minus two, gallops away and disappears into the distance, and then takes up the reins. He clucks his tongue at the harness animal on the right, encouraging it to step-up and pivot the wagon to the left. While the wagon turns, Griz notices the discarded cigar on the ground, still smoking. He reaches down and swipes it up from the roadway as the wagon points back toward town. Replacing his chewed cigar with the fresher one, Griz smiles to his escorts. "Well, hello gents. It's been a while…"

9

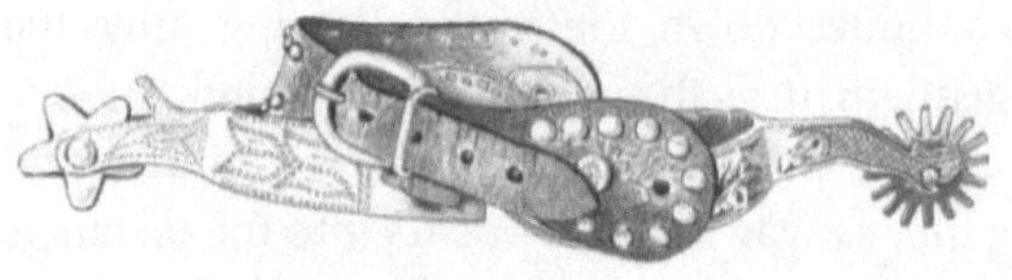

Traveling at a steady pace down the trail, Pack and Elliott ride side by side in silence, consumed by their own thoughts. The lingering odor from the latrine plunge still clings to Elliott's boots, and Pack catches a strong whiff on the breeze. He snorts, wipes his nose and moves his horse further away. She notices the increasing distance and looks over at him. "You really think we'll get some reward for just finding the money and returning it?"

"It's the Sheriff's responsibility to hunt for them fellas. The bank is the one who issues the reward for gettin' the money back."

Elliott shrugs and glances at the overstuffed saddlebags tied on behind Pack's saddle cantle. "What if they think it was us who took it?"

"Why would they think that?"

"Cause I found it in the crapper in town, and now we're riding back with it a day later."

"So?"

Pack thinks a moment, crinkles his brow and retorts, "Damn, Elliott... The way you talk makes it sound like you would just as well keep it!"

"I just want to look at all our options from this chance of fortune and keep an open mind."

The two ride along quietly, until Pack breaks the lull in conversation. "Did you see that posse headed out of town? They're gonna hunt them fellas 'till they drop. And, when they find 'em, they're gonna be mighty unhappy and come looking for what was took." He looks behind at the bulky, buckled-down saddlebags stuffed with the robbery money. "With this amount of cash at stake, every bounty hunter and lawman is going to be on the trail for it."

Gazing skyward, Elliott shrugs. "Not down in Mexico."

Dubious, her partner shakes his head. "Hell Elliott, Mexico is more'n a thousand miles from here."

"Just an option."

He looks over and studies her, a long while, before finally grimacing. "You're welcome to it since you were the one who found it, but I ain't looking to run the gauntlet and be watching over my shoulder for the rest of my days."

"I ain't sayin' anythin' that would leave you out."

"Then we return the robbery money to the bank."

"Okay… I'll stick with you, Pack."

~*~

A soft clomping of hooves steadily moves down the dirt roadway leading back toward the town. Pack rides along, lost in deep contemplation, as Elliott begins to squirm in the saddle. She turns to Pack. "I have to water the daisies"

"Ya mean, take a squirt?"

She nods, as he looks down the trail to see the trickles of telltale smoke from the town drifting over the treetops. "Dang Elliott. Can't it wait 'till town?"

She shakes her head and replies, "That's the exact spot what got us into this."

Mexico Sky

Nodding over to the grove of trees, Pack steers his horse off the main road. Elliott follows and, as she dismounts, tosses her bridle reins to Pack. She looks up at him as she starts to unbutton her new trousers and begins to squat. Suddenly uncomfortable, Pack looks toward the river nearby. "I'll water the horses 'til you're finished."

Watching him lead her mount away, Elliott grins, amused at Pack's shyness. Elliott squats against the trunk of a fallen tree and observes a small bird looking for a meal in the tall grass. Leaning against the log, with her back turned to the road, Elliott looks toward the stream in the valley where Pack lets the horses drink. She notices the tiny bird stop, look around, and then flit away when a rumbling is felt through the ground.

The thunder of horse hooves on the hard-packed road becomes louder as the posse approaches. With a quick wiggle and shake of her rear, Elliott pulls up her britches and swivels behind the fallen tree and looks over it. She ducks low, observing as the group of riders hurry past and out of sight.

~*~

Sitting beside a rock boulder at the edge of the stream, Pack waits and watches the two horses standing with their forelegs in the water as they drink. At the sound of rustling brush, he turns around to see Elliott scurrying down the steep hillside toward him. "What's with the hurry in yer gitty-up? You get stung by something?"

Nearly out of breath, Elliott stops and takes a moment to finally speak. "We got to go!"

"What is it?"

"While I was doin' my business, I saw a posse of a dozen or so men riding past, hell-bent for leather."

Reaching out to break a stick off a nearby tree branch, Pack taps his tall boot heel with the dead twig. "So what? They's out to find them two bank robbers."

Elliott appears anxious, reluctant to say any more. "Well, that's what I figured at first, but then I realized they was headed back toward town, not away from it."

Tossing the stick, Pack takes off his hat and scratches his head. "Hell, I don't know what they was doin'…"

Concerned, Elliott finally catches her breath and continues. "The posse we saw in town yesterday was headed in the other direction. They couldn't have doubled back and then gone too far south, unless they found something."

Frustrated by the thought of being chased by a posse, Pack puts on his hat and stares at the clear, running stream. His gaze travels over to the stuffed saddlebags on his horse and he frowns. "Jeez, Elliott... This is the reason why we need to git rid of that stolen money. There are crazy folks all over trying to find it and string up the ones who've got it."

"Sorry. It seemed like the thing to do at the time."

He adjusts the wide brim of his hat down and nods. "Heck, I would have done the same thing if someone was to throw all that loot my way." He looks down at her crap-smeared boots and gives an audible sniff. "Don't know if I would have crawled down in the shitter to get at it though." He stands up and she gives him a playful push.

Pack nearly tumbles over the bank and into the stream, but Elliot catches him. He regains his balance and turns to her. Elliott winks flirtingly at Pack. "Shucks Pack, you're the only one who I'll take any shit from."

10

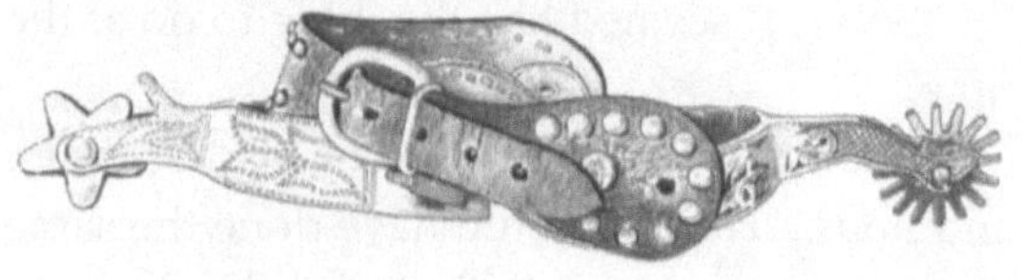

The main thoroughfare of town is a buzz of commotion. Horses and all sorts of wagons crowd the street. The stores and drinking establishments spill out all types of tough, western characters, from lawmen to bounty hunters and gamblers to gunfighters. Every citizen seems well-armed and ready for the hunt.

Riding into town with saddlebags noticeably empty, Pack and Elliott take in the lively pace of the once-quiet town. The two exchange a fleeting expression of awe and disbelief. Pack steers his horse toward a hitched wagon which several men load with food and supplies from the General Store. Stopping his horse an arm's length away, Pack leans down on his saddle horn and clears his throat to address one of them. "Eh, excuse me there fella… What's going on around here?" Pack glances around at the overwhelming amount of activity in town. "Was there a recent gold strike hereabouts?"

The man holds a sack of flour with a few boxes of rifle cartridges balanced on top. He barely breaks his stride, as he unloads his armful at the wagon box. "Gold strike? Hell, no! The bank was robbed yesterday, and there's forty thousand dollars of stolen money out there within a day's ride o' here."

"Forty thousand?"

Pack glances at Elliott, who patiently waits in the street, surrounded by the activity all around her. He turns back again as the man tucks the ammunition into the front of the wagon. "I thought it was twenty thousand?"

The man looks at Pack and curiously narrows an eye. "Damn, they're comin' from all over. You a bounty hunter?"

Putting on his friendliest expression, Pack sits up and raises his palms innocently. "No… Jest heard about it some."

The man accepts Pack's reply and steps aside from the wagon to continue his loading.

"Well, whatever it is, there is a pretty hefty reward put out for its return."

"What about them that took it?"

The man stops to observe the people getting ready in the street and tilts his head. "Dead or alive is what I hear."

"Dead or alive... For a bank holdup?"

The man pats his hand on the box of cartridges. "Yep. The reward money is said to be paid out whether the robbers are brought in upright or over a saddle."

Pack sits back against the cantle of his saddle seat and leans his hand on the flap cover of the empty saddle bag. "Ain't that chancy for folks?"

"It is if you're a bank robber."

Turning a shade paler, Pack looks around at the crowd in the street and then back to the man stepping up onto the raised boardwalk. "All these folks are here to find them who got the bank money?"

Flipping a casual wave as he heads back inside the store, the man calls over his shoulder, "For that kinda reward, you bet they are!"

~*~

Seated inside the nearly vacant saloon, Pack and Elliott watch the bustling crowds of reward-seekers filling the street. Pack sips from his beer, and Elliott rotates the handle of her frothy mug and mutters, "If I'd known all these folks would be lookin' for it, I'd a hid it a whole lot better."

Pack wipes his shirt sleeve to the drip of beer foam on his lip and looks across the table to her. "Hopefully someone will find where we stashed it and put an end to all of this." She looks a little sour at the potential loss of fortune and drinks from her glass. They both sit in silence a minute, until Elliott shakes her head, snorts and comments. "You know how you said we could drift down to Mexico someday?"

"Yeah… What of it?"

"Well, why the hell don't we?"

Pack looks at her over the rim of his beer mug, as he lifts it for another swallow. His eyes flit past her shoulder, and he lowers his voice. "With that stolen money, I suppose?"

Elliott turns to gaze outside the wide saloon doors at the full gamut of nefarious characters in the street, each out for the reward money and ready to kill their own mothers for it, or worse. She purses her lips and leans further forward on the table. "It ain't gonna be returned with the likes of these. Look at them… Not an honest-looking one in the bunch."

Nodding his head, Pack looks to several rough-looking customers having a drink at the bar, and then through the doorway at the multitude of heavily-armed bounty-hunters in the street. "Some innocent folk are sure to get hurt."

Tilting her chin in full agreement, Elliott continues, "You know it doesn't matter the amount of reward for it. There is no one in a hundred miles has got the moral foundation to do the right thing about that stolen money."

Pack follows Elliott's gaze around the room and turns to meet her bright eyes, as they finally come to rest on him. With a sigh, he shrugs. "I do."

11

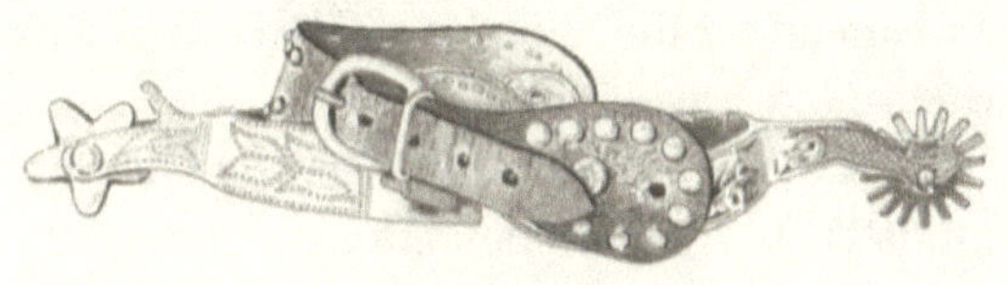

Slightly behind Pack, Elliott walks down the boardwalk to the sheriff's office, stepping past the reward-seeking predators as she goes. She moves up beside him and whispers softly. "Uh, Pack… You're just gonna tell 'em we found it?"

"Yeah."

"And you think the sheriff will believe you?"

"Why not?"

Elliott has to fall back, behind Pack a bit, as they maneuver through a cluster of men crowding the boardwalk. She moves up beside him again and grabs at his shirt sleeve.

"They're looking for two bank robbers and, the last time I counted, there were just two of us after splittin' from Griz."

Pack glances at Elliott, as he tugs his arm away and keeps walking toward the sheriff's office. "Not for a man and a woman..."

She stops in her tracks, coughs and pulls her hat down, as she sweeps her hair behind her ears under the wide brim. "I'm not exactly dressed like a woman!"

Pack stops to study her. He considers her unmistakable feminine curves under the mannish-style clothing and shrugs. "I'll just tell them the truth."

"Why would anyone believe you?"

Several townspeople push past them and reflexively wince at the stinking odor coming from Elliott's soiled boots. Pack notices them shirk aside and sniff at her fouled footwear. "Who else would have boots that smell as bad as yours do?" She hesitantly shakes her head at him and follows along when he continues on toward the sheriff's office.

~*~

A lineup of men on horseback waits for the sheriff. Along the front of the building, a wood bench is filled with an assortment of bounty-hunters expecting to gain an audience with the lawman. Pack makes his way past the long line of mercenaries and grabs for the handle of the front entry door. A boot kicks out firmly to block his entrance, followed by a gruff voice. "Hey bub… There is a line if you ain't noticed. You need to wait yer turn."

Pack looks at the bearded ruffian and offers up a smile. "I need to talk with the sheriff for a moment."

The tough-looking bounty-hunter stands up to the full measure of his height, much taller than Pack, and glowers. "No shit, stable-boy." He hooks his thumb over the buffalo robe on his shoulders and snarls. "Get in line like the rest."

Flushed with a good dose of embarrassment and anger, Pack drops his hand from the door handle and faces off with the man. The bigger man looms over him, and Pack scans the line of onlookers who stop their small talk and seem very interested in a poorly matched bout that could surely liven up the wait time. Pack tips the brim of his hat at the hulking man before him and nods. "Sorry, pal."

Stepping respectfully aside, Pack proceeds to the end of the line and finds an available spot on the long wood bench. Everyone snorts with disappointment, as Pack takes out his tobacco paper and fixin's, preparing to make himself a smoke. He glances over at the bounty-hunter again and grins sociably, until the man retakes his seat at the head of the line.

At the corner of the brick building, Elliott leans over to Pack as he finishes preparing his rolled tobacco. He swipes the paper across his tongue and offers it up to her. "Smoke?"

She declines the gesture, counts the menfolk in line before them and scratches the hair above the nape of her neck. "This is bullshit."

Pack tosses the cigarette to his lips and takes a matchstick from his upper vest pocket. "Yeah."

She gazes to the street at the men-for-hire waiting for their bounty papers. "Where did all this trash blow in from?" She watches Pack light the end of his cigarette and kick up a boot across his knee. "What're you thinking about, Pack?"

"Maybe pullin' a con."

In disbelief, Elliott looks to him with astonishment. "You're not serious! In this crowd?"

He shrugs, takes a drag and blows out a smoke ring. "Why not? They like to gamble more'n most."

She nods her head in total agreement and murmurs, "Yeah, with their lives. There are more guns in this town today than in one of Sam Colt's factories."

"At least it's somewhat honest work."

Elliott looks at Pack like he's gone nutty and remarks, "More honest than finding a jackpot in the shithouse?"

"A safer bet."

"I disagree."

"You would."

"Why do you say that?"

"Ever since we ran into Hank..." Their whispered conversation is interrupted by the sheriff exiting the office, followed by the mysterious gentleman who led the posse.

Elliott watches as the two men cordially shake hands. She suddenly recognizes the man from the group of horseback riders that rode past her, while she was relieving herself near the creek. She delivers a sharp elbow jab to Pack's ribs, and he chokes on his inhaled smoke. As she motions for him to follow, he sputters, "What is it?"

"We gotta go."

Pack looks down at the remainder of his cigarette and tosses it away. "We'll lose our place in line."

Elliott tugs her hat down on her head and raises her coat collar to conceal her face from the sheriff and associate. She starts to walk away and hisses back at her partner, "Dammit Pack… You're gonna lose a lot more'n that if'n you don't follow me."

Irritated by her recurring elusiveness, Pack gets to his feet, scans the line of waiting men and follows after Elliott. The mysterious gentleman glances in their direction briefly, before turning back and continuing his conversation with the officer of the law.

12

Standing by her horse, Elliott digs through her saddlebag, looking for something. Pack walks up behind her and leans on the hitching-post rail by his own tethered mount. He wipes his hand under his nose and shakes his head. "I surely don't know what's been goin' on with you lately, but this mysterious behavior is wearin' on me."

She glances at him before continuing to look in her bag. "The Sheriff is not the guy we need to confess and turn ourselves in to, in this town."

"Why is that? You'd rather it be a preacher?"

Elliott looks up at Pack and gives him a sarcastic smile. "I ain't so foolish to think I could ever get you in front of a durned preacher." He looks at her oddly, as she continues, "The gentleman he was talking to outside the jailhouse was the same man who was leading those riders toward town."

"So?"

At a loss, she stares at her partner. "So... Something didn't seem right with them two talking."

"Jeez Elliott... What the hell is going on with you? You're the only thing that doesn't seem right."

Elliott fastens down the buckle straps on her saddlebag, peeks over the rump of her horse and blurts, "Oh shit..."

Pack leans back on the hitching rail, removes his hat and scratches his head. "What is it now?"

"It's Griz."

"What about 'im?"

He puts his hat back on and moves around the horses. He stands next to Elliott and they both watch Griz, just in front of a two rider chaperons, drive the wagon into town. Pack is about to step forward to confront him, when Elliott grabs his arm and whispers, "What's he doing here?"

"I was just going to ask 'im."

"Look who's with him."

Pack stops and waits. As the pair of riders comes out from behind the wagon, he recognizes both Hank and Fisk. Taking a step back between their saddle horses, Pack and Elliott watch the riders come up alongside the wagon and escort Griz toward the sheriff's office. Pack tilts his head down and blocks Elliott's view, as Fisk rides by with Griz's short-barreled shotgun cradled across his saddle pommel.

In disbelief, Pack turns to stare at Elliott and utters. "What the hell is this about?!?"

As Elliott leans out to watch the wagon and riders approach the crowd in front of the sheriff's office, she replies, "I don't know, but your ol' pal Hank seems to be talkin' real familiar to that fancy-dressed gentleman with the sheriff."

"What do you mean, my old pal?"

Elliott smiles harmlessly at Pack and then looks away. They watch as Hank steps from his horse, gives a few instructions to Fisk, and then goes inside with the gentleman talking with the sheriff. Fisk raises the double-barreled shotgun toward Griz and motions for him to climb down from the wagon. They walk through the crowd in front of the sheriff's office and follow the others into the building.

With a cough, Pack looks to Elliott. "Whose old pal?" She turns to face Pack and he tilts his head toward the office. "Hank seemed to put on that he knew you from way back."

She breaks the moment of mutual discomfort by responding tersely. "I've known a lot of fellers who I don't brag to you about." Irritated, Pack seems ready to reply, but instead he keeps his mouth shut. Elliott waits for some kind of pithy retort before looking back to the group in front of the sheriff's office. "So, are we going to figure out how to rescue Griz, or do you want to discuss my past social encounters?"

Flustered, Pack shakes his head and waves her toward the alleyway leading behind the jailhouse. "C'mon, Elliott! Let's go find out about Griz."

~*~

Seated on a jail cell bunk, Griz waits in the back portion of the sheriff's office. He leans comfortably against the wall, and listens to the quiet murmur of voices in the front room. From the barred window high above him, a hand-full of gritty sand comes drizzling down. He dusts off his head and puts his hat on while cursing, "Gol-damn! What the hell?"

As Griz wipes the particles of grit from his grey whiskers, he hears a quiet voice from the high window. "Psst… Griz." He glances up to the secured window opening and stares at it curiously until he hears another faint whisper. "Griz, you in there?" Climbing onto the frame of the cell bunk, the old-timer looks out the small window to the evening sky and sees Elliott peeking in, as she holds onto the window sill.

"Hey, kiddo. What're you doin' here?"

"We're wanting to know the same from you."

"They're lookin' for you."

"Who is?"

Griz can only see the top of her head as she clings to the window sill. "That feller inside is a special agent of sorts… Maybe a Pinkerton or some other such thing. He put a special posse together to hunt for you both."

"Did you tell him about the money?"

"Somehow they already figured you had it."

He stands on his toes to watch her through the window, as she sways a bit while keeping a firm hold on the sill. "You okay out there, missy? Where's Pack?"

~*~

Outside the high window of the jailhouse, Elliott stands awkwardly on Pack's shoulders. He braces himself on the wall and looks up to the window. "Hey, Griz! I'm down here." Elliott wobbles again and replants her soiled boot heels on his supporting shoulders. As he cringes at the awful smelling stench, she whispers down to him. "Stop moving down there, or I'm gonna fall."

The encrusted shaft of her boot rubs against Pack's cheek, and his face contorts with disgust. As he braces himself better against the exterior wall, he glances up at the curving seat-bottom of her riding trousers. Without thinking too much about it, he mumbles, "Why did I pick a female partner who never wears a dress?" Pac restrains himself from picturing Elliott in a dress, when she looks down at him and asks, "What was that?"

"Nothing… Just hurry it up."

She looks in again to the top portion of Griz's face. "Why did they bring you back into town?"

"They were lookin' for you."

Elliott nearly falls from the window sill and grouses at Pack below her. "Stop shufflin' around down there, will ya!"

Still perched on the cell bunk, Griz listens to them banter outside, and he then hears someone approaching from the front office. "Shhhh, you two..." Listening intently, he waits and then hears voices again, nearer this time. "Kiddo, it's not safe fer you two around here."

"We'll get you out of there."

Griz holds onto the window sill and glances over his shoulder at the door to the outer office. He looks back outside and mutters, "Don't worry 'bout me. They'll have to let me go eventually. Food isn't bad, or at least not worse than my own cooking." Returning his attention to the front office, Griz listens again and whispers, "They're coming. Go on 'n git."

13

The bright glow from a lantern appears under the door, as a key turns in the lock. Griz steps down from the bunk and sits on the front edge just as the illuminated forms of the sheriff and posse leader open the door to the jail cell, holding area. The sheriff stares at Griz through the vertical bars and grins. "Hey there old-timer. You ready to talk yet?"

Holding up the lantern, he looks to the gentleman beside him and then to Hank, who trails in behind them. "He'll talk sooner or later. These old fellas with not a lot of years left don't want to finish them locked in a metal cage." The sheriff grips one of the vertical cell bars and gives it a rattle for emphasis.

Indifferent, Griz stares at them and remains seated. "This is the most comfortable I've been in some years." Glancing upward to the darkening sky through the window, he yawns and stretches his arms. "I's got fresh air, reg'ler vittles and a bed that don't smell too half-bad." He pats the mattress and a puff of dust rises into the glow of the lantern. "What would you fellas like to talk about?"

The leader of the posse steps forward to study Griz a moment before finally speaking. "We would like to know where your saddle-mates absconded to."

"Like I told you before... They was jest gone."

Turning away slightly, the gentleman politely asks, "Sheriff, may I have some time alone with this detainee?" With a slight flick of his wrist, a shiny knife blade suddenly appears in his palm below his sleeve. No one seems to notice the secret blade except Griz.

Uneasy, the sheriff turns his gaze from the gentleman at the bars to Griz. "Uh, I don't think so. We'll give him another day, and then you can do whatever."

The knife blade stealthily slides back up the man's coat sleeve as the mysterious gentleman regards Griz with hawk-like scrutiny. With a wickedness that nearly makes the old-timer squirm, the gentleman at the bars glares at his prey. "We'll talk more soon, I'm sure."

Standing behind them, Hank silently watches the tense exchange. From his vantage point, Hank notices Griz glance to the high window, and directs his gaze outside. In the dusky, evening light, Hank can barely make out the tips of some fingers gripping the sill. He quickly shifts his attention away, as the sheriff bangs his fist against the jail bars and speaks to his prisoner. "Alright feller, you have until tomorrow noon, to tell us where your pals are off to, or then I'll turn over your custody to this gentleman's outfit."

With a grunt, Griz flops on the cot to a relaxed position. He waves at a cloud of dust and settles in to get comfortable. "The benefit of being a feller my age is I don't really have to worry much about tomorrow." Holding the lantern up high, the sheriff ushers the visitors from the jail cell portion of the office and Hank glimpses up to the window sill one last time.

~*~

In the back alley, Pack looks up to where Elliott clings to the window ledge. "What's going on up there?"

"Shh…"

Pack sweats and grimaces at the strain of supporting her weight on his aching shoulders. As he stands with his hands planted firmly on the adobe brick wall, he hears the distinctive click of a pistol hammer, being cocked. Turning his head slightly aside, Pack notices the smiling face of his old associate, Fisk. He lowers his gaze to see the single-action revolver directed at him, as Fisk laughingly mutters, "What'cha doing there, Pack?"

The sound of cowboy boots crunching on gravel turns Pack's attention beyond Fisk. Craning his neck, he sees Hank. The smarter half of the scheming pair puts his hands to his hips and shakes his head admonishingly. "Hey there Packey, ol' pardner. Appears someone got caught with his hand in the cookie jar…"

Leaving Elliott to dangle from the window sill, Pack steps out from underneath her. He stands upright, flexes his shoulders and faces them both. "Hello there, Hank… Fisk." Beside him, Elliott kicks out her boots to get a supporting foothold and bangs her knees against the jail's outer wall. "What the hell...?"

Fisk keeps his pistol aim raised and held steady, while Hank watches Pack position himself to grab at his sidearm. "Now hold on there, Pack... Don't go gettin' the wrong idea." Hank gives a sly sort of a wink. "We're here to help you."

Elliott's legs continue to kick out as she scrapes her toes on the crumbling adobe wall. "Pack, I'm gonna fall..."

Ignoring the flapping of legs beside him, Pack lets his gaze drift over to Fisk, who still directs a cocked firearm at him. "Now, what would be the wrong idea?"

With his hands held up chest level, away from his gun, Hank takes a step closer and nearly whispers toward Pack, "That we want to take that robbery money away from you."

Pack holds to his readied position against the wall, studying the pair as Elliott's legs flail and kick alongside him. "What is it that you want, exactly?"

"We just want to help you turn that stolen money in. That's what you're back here in town to do ain't it?"

Surprised, Fisk looks to Hank and shakes his head. "They ain't that stupid as to turn that money in, are they?"

Hank casts an irritated gaze to his partner. "Shut up, Fisk..." Offering a friendly smile, he looks back to Pack and Elliott, "We know you have the money, and maybe the burden of it is jest too much for two honest folks like you to handle?"

Shaking his head, Pack glances to Elliott's dangling feet, then replies. "We don't have it anymore."

As street lamps are being lit throughout the town, Hank takes a step closer, out of the dimness, and into a glowing shaft of orange light. His eyes seem to flicker with a fiery-glow as he speaks. "Well, I'll bet you know where it is."

Finally, Elliott releases her grip on the window sill and drops to the ground with a thud, beside Pack. "Gol-durnit Pack! Why the heck did ya leave me hangin'?" She shakes her sore hands and flexes her fingers, as she looks up to see Fisk with his gun out and Hank looming close. "Hello Hank... Long-time, no see."

14

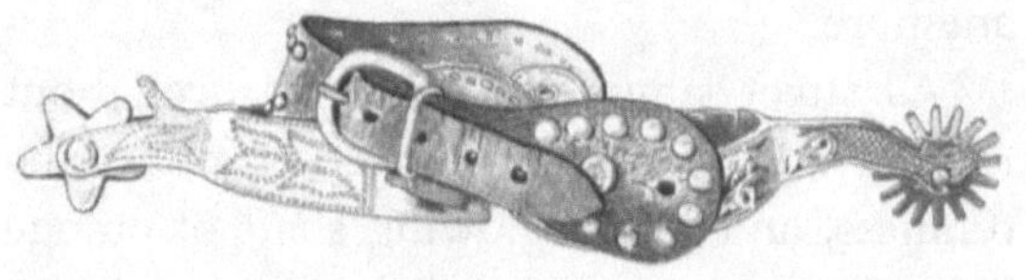

The morning rays of sunlight shine through the hazy, dust-filled interior of the livery barn. While saddling their horses, Pack and Elliott watch each other's backs as Hank and Fisk gather their gear nearby. Elliott leans toward Pack and whispers, "You actually trust them two to turn the money in?"

Pack continues at his task and keeps his voice low. "Nope, but I think they'll be able to get Griz out of that jail."

"Yeah, I guess that's the important thing."

Hank breaks from what he's doing, and walks over to them when he notices the confidential conversation going on. He puts on a pleasant smile while suspiciously eyeing them. "You two ain't scheming about how to be rid of me, are ya?"

Elliott returns his bogus grin with a sarcastic retort. "Why no, Hank. We really do enjoy yer company and the leverage you got on us."

Hank pretends hurt in return, and cozies up to Elliott. "Sweetie, when we saw each other in the saloon the other day, we knew we were gonna be working together again soon." Hank notices that Pack is irritated by his familiarity with Elliott, so he turns it up a notch. "Everyone can benefit in this here situation and no one even gets hurt. Okay there honey?" He winks to Pack for approval, gets closer to Elliott and adds, "Ain't that the way you like to do it... So no one gets hurt?"

Uncomfortable with the way Hank is reading him, Pack turns to his horse and tightens the cinch ring on the saddle. He speaks over his shoulder while inspecting his stirrup strap. "Sure, Hank. Let's get Griz out of hock 'nd go git the money."

Hank reaches out and slaps Pack on the shoulder, as he smiles at Elliott. "Who knows? This partnership may last!"

Glaring at him, Elliott responds, "Why would it?"

Hank takes a step closer to her, and puts his other arm out to the horse's flank, blocking Elliott between himself and her mount. "We once worked well together and could again."

She notices Fisk's expression of surprise and whispers loudly enough for him to overhear, "But, what about Fisk?"

Hank doesn't understand until his partner calls out, "Hey Hank! What are y'all saying over there?" Coming over to the rest of the group, Fisk keeps a nervous hand on the butt of his holstered revolver as he asks again, "What are y'all talkin' about without me?"

Elliott uses the brief distraction to slip under Hank's extended arm and away from him. He smiles, as he watches Elliott evade him by moving around to the other side of her horse and nearer to Pack. "Jest discussing the plan is all."

Observing the contentious vibe between them, Fisk starts to get suspicious. "Did somethin' change?"

Pack turns from adjusting his saddle cinch to address Fisk. "Nothin' changed. We'll have the horses ready behind the hotel when you bring Griz through."

Fisk narrows both his eyes at Pack and then at Elliott. "Remember... We get the money, or one of you gets shot."

Elliott retorts, "How could we forget that part?"

Hank shoves Fisk aside and reprimands his partner. "Hey now… No need for that kind of talk. We have a good, trusting partnership, and we don't want anything to spoil it." He looks to Pack and then to Elliott. "We follow the plan as discussed, and then everyone fulfills their end of the bargain." Hank stares at them and waits for their acknowledgement.

Pack glances aside to Elliott and lowers his chin. "That's right. You turn in the bank's money, and the full reward is yours."

Swinging into her saddle, Elliott peers down at Fisk and takes notice that he still doesn't seem all that trusting. "Alright boys, enough with the chit-chat. Let's go 'n git to it."

Pack steps around his horse and hands Elliott another set of reins for a mount intended for Griz. He turns to Hank. "Yer mounts set and ready to go?"

"You bet, pardner." Hank glances at Fisk and confirms the arrangement. "If everyone sticks to the plan, all should turn out jest fine."

Pack mounts up and adjusts the leather reins through his gloved fingers. "Good. We'll be waitin' behind the hotel." He nudges his horse past Fisk, rides to the fence rail, and unties the tethers on the saddle mounts for Hank and Fisk.

Hank glances over to Elliott, who turns away. Then he tips his hat brim in salute to Pack. "See y'all on the back side." He pats one of their horses on the rump and, along with Fisk, struts out through the wide-open doors of the livery barn.

15

In the light of a new day, the street is still bustling with the horse traffic of Johnny-come-lately bounty-hunters. Outside the sheriff's office, there is a new batch of faces waiting for official wanted-papers on recapturing the stolen bank money. The front door opens and Hank steps outside followed by Griz and then Fisk. They cross the boardwalk and step down to the street, before the sheriff appears in the office doorway. "I will expect him back by evenin'. If not, we'll come git 'im, and won't be friendly about it."

Turning in the street, Hank looks up at the sheriff. "Sure thing. We shouldn't have any difficulties with him."

The sheriff hesitates a second, lifts up a hand and calls, "Hold on there a moment. I'll send one of my boys with ya." He looks to one of the badge-wearing deputies standing near the entryway and waves him along after the prisoner escort. "Joe, go along with 'em and make sure our honored guest is returned here by dusk."

With an assenting wave of his hand to signal his reply, the deputy moves away from his spot on the wall. "Yes, sir." He hops from the boardwalk and falls in behind the prisoner. Fisk is irritated when he is ushered aside as the deputy moves into position next to Griz.

Hank offers a waving gesture to the sheriff and continues across the busy street. "Thanks a lot, Sheriff."

~*~

In the back alley, Elliott sits horseback, while Pack stands at the hotel's rear porch. She holds the mounts and watches him keep his attention inside the open back door. Taking a gander to the empty saddles on the horses beside her, she shakes her head and calls to her partner, "You know, they're gonna try and screw us over at some point…"

"Yeah… Probably…"

"What are we gonna to do about it?"

He looks back at her and shrugs. "Don't know… Depends on things. First thing, is to git Griz out of jail." Elliott waits on her horse and watches Pack return his attention inside, to where he can see the hotel's lobby.

From her vantage point, Elliott can almost see directly through the opened lobby doors to the street. Fidgeting in the saddle, she asks, "What do you think about that guy who was questioning Griz? You recognize his voice?"

Pack peeks back and smirks. "I couldn't hear him too well from my spot as the bottom rung of the ladder."

"I don't know… Something seemed familiar."

"Ask your pal Hank. He seemed to know him."

Slightly perturbed at Pack's snide answer, Elliott wiggles her chin. "Askin' him about the truth is like talkin' to you about feelings."

Turning back to look at her inquisitively, he grunts and asks, "Feelings for what?"

"Anything."

Pack snorts, "Well, I *feel* like getting Griz and clearing the hell out of this place."

Grinning, Elliott can't help but point out the obvious. "That's exactly what we did yesterday."

Pack, at a loss for words, lets his mouth hang open, until he catches a glimpse of Griz being escorted across the street by their two associates and a deputy.

~*~

At the wide front porch of the hotel, Griz follows Hank up the steps to the entrance, glancing at the deputy and Fisk following behind. He casually mutters, "No need to move me up in accommodations. I was sleeping jest fine where I was."

As he passes through the hotel's double entry doors, Hank looks to the back door and grand staircase in the lobby. His gaze travels upward, just as the mysterious gentleman and three members of his posse start to descend the stairway. He curses under his breath. "Oh, shit..."

Clustered behind Hank, the deputy keeps close to Griz as Fisk looks nervously out to the back. On the main staircase, the well-dressed gentleman leading his group down the stairs abruptly looks at Hank, then at Griz standing directly behind. He pauses midway down the staircase and utters to Hank, "What is this all about?"

Hank quickly responds, "Sir, we thought you might want to question him alone in your room?" The posse leader continues down the wide staircase, stopping at the final stair to ponder the peculiar scenario.

Holding Griz firmly by the elbow, the deputy moves toward him. "You didn't request to see the prisoner?"

"No. We were just on our way to see him."

They turn to Hank, who smiles sheepishly. "Sorry… My mistake."

The deputy keeps his grip on Griz and reaches out to push Hank. "C'mon, buddy… You're going to explain all this to the sheriff."

Seeing his partner get shoved backward to the entry, Fisk immediately draws his handgun, cocks it and fires a shot. "Get outta the way Hank! I got 'em!" The deputy takes the shot in the upper thigh, spins away from Griz, and lands on the lobby floor.

As he and his men step from the stairway, the gentleman is about to speak, when Hank suddenly slams his fist into the man's jaw. The leader of the posse reels back from the surprising blow and tumbles toward the hotel's front desk. The clerk at the counter catches him, and they fall against the service bell, causing it to ring. The three members of the posse each take out their pistols and fire.

Griz drops to the carpeted floor and rolls himself outside through the front entryway doors to the hotel porch. Hank and Fisk dash for cover behind furniture, while random shots are fired in all directions. Flaming muzzle blasts crisscross the lobby and fill the air with a thick cloud of black-powder smoke.

~*~

Pack stands at the rear exit of the hotel and can hardly believe what he is seeing. He watches Griz roll out the front doorway, while hastily fired bullets tear through the lobby. He turns to Elliott standing in her saddle stirrups to see better inside. The cluster of saddled mounts, uneasy from the sound of gunshots, starts to skitter away from the porch.

Spurs jangling, Pack makes a running leap from the hotel's rear stoop and lands directly on his horse's back. He pulls his reins from Elliott's grasp and backs his horse away. "Elliott! Git them other horses to the front!"

Gripping the leads of the other mounts, Elliott spurs her horse onward and around the side of the hotel building. As she rounds the corner, horses in tow, she sees Pack draw his gun as he charges his horse up the porch stairway and in through the hotel's rear entrance.

~*~

Emerging from the alley with the getaway horses trailing behind, Elliott rides into the street fronting the hotel. Gun-smoke billows from the opened doors, and clouds up the windows as the shots continue to erupt from inside the lobby. She watches Griz tumble all the way to the bottom step of the porch. She breathes a sigh of relief as he sits up, uninjured, and dusts himself off. "Dammit, Griz!" she yells. "Get yer ass over here and mount up."

The old-timer climbs to his feet, shuffles over to one of the anxious horses and pulls himself up to the empty saddle. "This was some damn rescue..." Griz smiles at her, adding, "Was this his idea?"

Elliott frowns just as Pack charges horseback through the hotel lobby firing off his pistol toward the main desk and stairs. "Yep, jest like old times."

Guiding his mount through the wide, double doorway, Pack urges the horse to cross the wooden deck and leap off the hotel's broad porch steps. Reining his horse to a skidding halt alongside Griz and Elliott, he notices the look on their faces and exclaims. "This was not a part of my plan!"

Several more blasts of gunfire erupt as Fisk hurries out of the hotel and jumps to the street, dashing for one of the empty horses. He grabs the saddle horn while the animal circles in panic, puts a foot to the open stirrup and swings up. Elliott tosses him the reins for both mounts, and he grabs the headstall of the last horse. Hank tumbles through an open window and quickly regains his feet. Fisk guides the saddled horse over to the porch railing and calls, "Hank! Over here!"

Trying to keeping his horse under control, Pack reloads his six-gun from the row of cartridges on his gun-belt, as he ushers Griz and Elliott out of town. "Go on 'nd git, already! Head out, and we'll catch up with you at the meeting spot." They both sink spur and steer around the confusion in the street, as men, horses and wagons try to evade the gunfire that comes zinging from the hotel.

On the hotel's front veranda, Hank fires one last round into the smoke-filled lobby, then puts a foot to the porch rail and side-vaults into the saddle of the last available mount. Giving cover fire, Pack snaps off a pistol shot at one of the posse members, causing the door to splinter as the man ducks back into hiding. Fisk tosses Hank the reins to his horse, and they follow after Pack and the others to the far end of town.

16

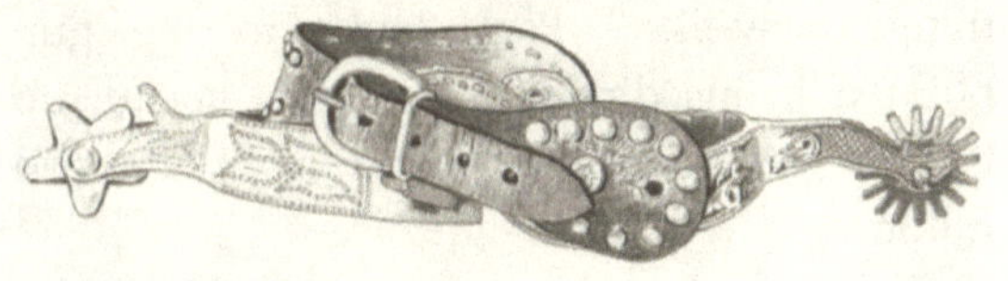

A good distance beyond the town, Pack slows his horse to a trot, letting Hank and Fisk catch up and ride alongside him. The pair of riders laughs apprehensively between themselves. Pack glares at Hank and grumbles, "What the hell was that?"

In response, Hank turns the barrel of his pistol up and starts to dump the empty shell casings from the cylinder. "Lighten up! Everything worked out fine..."

"The hell it did! That was a shootin' gallery!"

Fisk merely shrugs and glances back down the road. Hank, snickering as he loads some fresh cartridges, asks, "First time shooting your way out of a town?"

"Dammit! That's not the point... We were supposed to get Griz, easy-like, and ride out unnoticed."

Pointing his firearm out to the side, Hank grimaces. "What's yer problem, Pack? We done got Griz out, and we're gonna keep things easy-like." Pack looks to the gun pointed in his direction and then ahead, up the trail, to where they follow after Griz and Elliott.

Before he has time to respond, Fisk rides up close alongside Pack and quickly grabs the pistol from his holster. Pack's first impulse is to grab for his gun back, but Fisk thumbs back the hammer and aims it at him. "That's right... Let's just keep things easy-like, and no one gets hurt."

With a look of disgust, Pack glances toward Hank. "Was this the plan all along?"

"Nope, but sure don't hurt to have some insurance." They continue to ride along, watching the trail ahead for the others. Fisk uncocks the hammer on Pack's gun and lowers it from view. Hank keeps the horses crowded together, with Pack crammed in the middle, and nudges him with his elbow. "We're gonna ride along easy, catch up with ol' Griz 'nd Elliott, git that money and be on our way."

Staring forward, up the road, Pack shakes his head. "Did either of you ever plan on turnin' it in?"

Fisk lets out a laugh. "Sometimes you sure are dumb." Hank merely smiles as he continues watching down the path with Pack at his side.

~*~

In the middle of the road, Elliott and Griz wait for the others to catch up. In front of the saddle horn, tied together with a rope, the two soiled bags of money are draped across Elliott's horse. Murmuring aloud, Griz looks over at the filthy sacks as he scratches the coarse whiskers under his chin. "Elliott, you know them two cain't be trusted…"

Elliott adjusts her seat and looks solemn as she waits. "Yeah, but what other choice do we have?"

"I don't know. I ain't what you'd call the thinkin' one, but Pack would have some idea for an edge."

She gazes down at the money sacks, "We just want this over and done with, so we can head down the trail in peace."

Unsure, Griz tilts his head and spits past his boot toe. "Hmm… I don't know if that's gonna happen after what's all gone on in town of late."

Concerned, Elliott ruminates about the mysterious gentleman and then about partnering up with Hank and Fisk. "We have to at least try."

"I ain't saying we don't try, jest that Pack'd have a much bett'r plan than this 'Wait 'n see!' that we're doin' now."

"Any ideas, Griz?"

"Like I said, I ain't the brains of this outfit."

Elliott looks up from the money across her pommel and sniffs to clear her nose of the foul odor from the filthy sacks. She takes off her hat, sweeps her hair back and thinks. Turning to look at the old man beside her, she cracks a grin. "Griz, how do you feel about Mexico?"

~*~

At the stand of trees near the road, Pack rides up with Hank close beside and Fisk coming along, slightly behind. Elliott sits on her horse, alone, as the men peer into the dimness of the grove. Fisk keeps Pack's gun in hand, as he looks for Griz. "Where's the old man?"

Suspicious, Hank looks at his partner and then to Pack. "No tricks now, or I'll be sure to have Fisk shoot her first." Pack nods his understanding, as he looks to the trees for

Griz. They stop their horses, three abreast, and stand before Elliott. Hank looks around and puts on a smile. "Hello sweetheart. Where's 'ol Griz?" His eyes lower to the bags tied on her saddle. "That the money?"

Elliott sits tall in the saddle, keeping a careful eye on the men before her. "You boys get outta town okay?"

Pack moves his eyes deliberately toward Fisk, so only she can see, and grunts. "Just the usual."

Noticing his shifty eyes, Elliott looks at him strangely. "You okay there, Pack?"

"Yeah... Go ahead, and give 'em the money."

"They still gonna turn it in?"

Shifting in his saddle, Hank interrupts their chat. "Now darlin', you know me from a long ways back..."

Quick as a flash, Elliott draws, cocks and aims her pistol. "Yeah, I know you. Pack, ride over here."

Just about to ride ahead, Pack halts at the sound of another revolver clicking beside him. Fisk, holding a pistol aimed at Pack's chest, clears his throat. "Not so fast, bucko!"

Elliott notices Fisk pointing Pack's own pistol at him. "Is that *your* shooter, Pack?"

Pack shrugs and nods his head with a look of shame. "He took it a ways back." Suddenly, Pack swings and belts Fisk across the mouth, nearly knocking him from the saddle. Recovering quickly, Fisk raises the cocked gun toward Pack. He pulls the trigger to the sound of an empty *click*. Elliott still has her pistol raised toward them, as Pack reaches out to grab his own handgun by the barrel and pull it away from Fisk. "Give me that you dirty son-of-a…" He urges his horse over to Elliott and begins reloading his revolver.

Impressed, Hank whistles through his teeth and glances over to Fisk sucking on a swollen lip. "I'll be danged. Pretty gutsy there, and quite the gamble. In all the confusion, ya know, I wasn't even sure if I fired all six or only five."

Relieved to be with her saddle partner again, Elliott keeps her pistol trained on Hank, while also keeping a watchful eye on Fisk. In defense of Pack, she puffs her chest. "Fellas, you know that he ain't ever been to a town that he didn't have to fire all six to get out of."

Pack gives Elliott a sidelong glance. "Thanks…" He finishes reloading the pistol, gives the gun a twirl and drops it back into the holster at his hip. "Now, we want to go peaceful, and we don't expect to ever see you fellas again."

Shaking his head, Hank lets his gaze travel down to the money bags on Elliott's horse. "Hardly…"

Following his attention to the pair of robbery sacks, Pack reaches over and pulls them from Elliott's saddle horn. He holds them out to Hank and then, thinking better of it, tosses them to the ground. "You do whatever yer gonna do with this or git the reward for it… We'll be on our way."

Utterly dumbfounded, Elliott shakes her head. "Uhh, hey partner… Shouldn't we have discussed that exchange?"

Pack turns his horse away and walks past the sacks. "Nope. We're done with it."

Smiling with satisfaction, Hank waves goodbye to Pack and offers a broad wink to Elliott. "Now that's fine by me." He notices her look remorsefully at the soiled bags of money. Glimpsing over her shoulder, he watches Pack riding away and offers, "Feel free to stick around, sweetheart."

Overhearing Hank's amorous offer, Pack halts his horse, pauses, and then looks back to Elliott. "C'mon, Elliott. Let's go." She tucks her chin, glances down at the bags one more time and turns her horse to follow Pack.

Eagerly jumping down from his horse, Fisk grabs up the two tethered bank sacks and instantly crinkles his nose. "Dang, these money bags smell like shit!"

Hank smiles happily and lets out a shrewd chuckle. "Cain't smell any worse than workin' with rustled livestock." He squints through the evening light, as Pack and Elliott move off down the road and slowly disappear into the distance. Watching Fisk toss the money bags over the front of his saddle and mount up, Hank murmurs, "Well damn, imagine that... Choosing a riding companion over an easy grab of dough?"

17

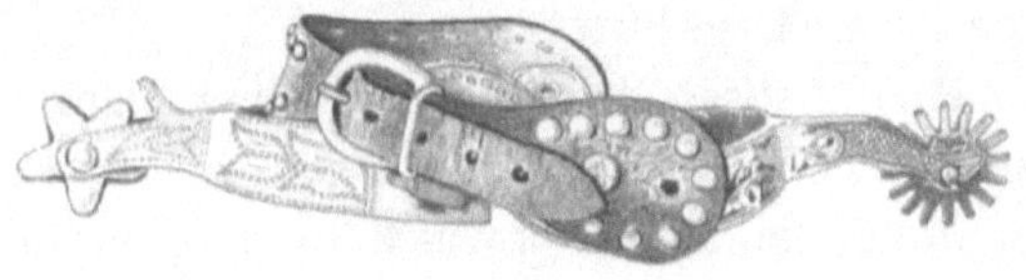

Pack and Elliott travel silently along the moonlit path. Occasionally they stop to listen for anyone following on their back-trail. Pack gazes up through the trees to the starry sky and breathes a sigh of relief. "I'm glad to be clear of them."

"For now, at least…"

He looks over at her curiously and tries to make out her features in the darkness. "Where's Griz?"

"He'll meet us at the river crossing in a few days." Elliott keeps her hat brim tilted low to keep the mischievous twinkle in her eye from catching his attention.

"Good plannin'. Gettin' Griz out of there, makin' them uncertain if they were in the sights of a rifle."

"Yeah, well, I figured he'd need a head start."

"He should be fine. He's mounted well."

Giving her horse a prodding touch with her heels, Elliott moves ahead on the roadway. "Let's hurry it up a bit."

Pack pauses to listen, and then glances around at the darkened features of the mountain landscape. "I was thinkin' of findin' a place to get some rest."

"Not tonight... We need to make some distance."

After a short, jaunting trot, Pack catches his horse up to Elliott, reaches out and grabs a hold of her horse's bridle. Slowing his mount to a stop in front of her, he stares at her curiously while retaining his hold on the headstall of her horse. "What's goin' on, Elliott?"

"We need to meet up with Griz."

"He'll be fine... Won't he?" Elliott is quiet and keeps her face partly concealed in the shadows. Pack studies her a moment, until he gradually realizes what she's done. "Dammit, Elliott! What was in those bags?"

She drops her chin to her chest, looks up and quietly murmurs in response, "Some river rocks and soiled britches."

Pack lowers his head in defeat, and releases her horse. He breathes deeply to even his temper before looking over to her. "Whatever made you think that was a good idea?"

"Griz agreed that they might harm us otherwise."

In the dim light, he can't see clearly enough to make out the expression on her features or what she is thinking. "You realize that they surely want to do us harm now?"

"Only if they find us..."

Pack sways his head and grumbles in disgust. "Jeez... You still stuck on goin' to Mexico?"

"They won't find us down there."

"That's a long ways..."

"Well, let's git to it then."

Elliott steers her horse to move around Pack, but he blocks her path and stares at her with a burning intensity that transcends the darkness. "I want to get one thing clear."

"Yes, Pack?"

"This is it... We've gone too far, and we can't return the money now. I want it understood that if we both survive, there will never be another time. We don't rob and steal… Elliott, I don't want that type of lifestyle, or what it brings."

She nods her head and tugs at the front of her hat brim. "Agreed. I'll stick with you, Pack."

After a moment of silence, Pack turns to look down the long, dark road before them. "Alright… Let's head south."

~*~

As the sunshine beams through the trees, the pounding hooves from a large crowd of approaching horses are heard. In the early morning chill, Hank and Fisk steer their mounts away from the roadway and wait. Fisk, sporting a fattened lip, leans over to Hank and whispers, "You suppose it's them?"

"That fella ain't quitin' till he hunts them down."

"What about us?"

Hank looks over at his partner and tilts his head. "Yeah? What about us?"

"You kind of rearranged his nose in the hotel."

Hank sits back to quietly listen again, and realizes that the posse is almost upon them. "If he comes after me, I'll shoot him the next time. The busted beak was just a warning."

From their hidden position, the two hold their mounts in check, as the posse of horsemen comes down the pathway and thunders past.

18

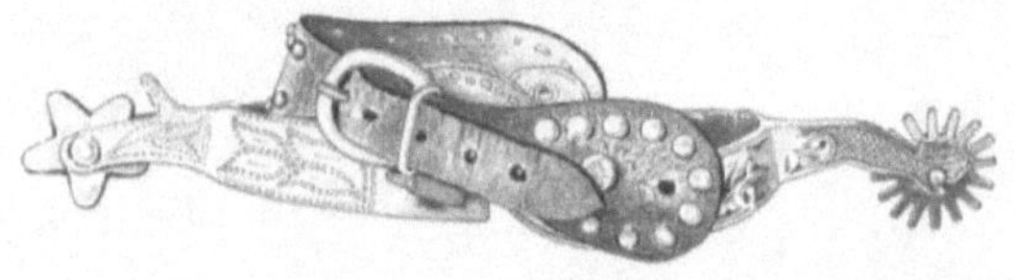

A ferry-caretaker's ramshackle shack sits next to the river with a transport raft tethered to the nearby bank. While riding up to the small, wooden structure, Pack and Elliott gaze around for any sign of Griz. The boatman comes out of the shack and into the morning sun, smoking a pipe and squinting in their direction. "Haloo, there…"

The two riders split, as Pack moves toward the boatman and Elliott steers down the grassy slope to the river. Pack stops before the hermit-like river-rat and sociably pushes back his hat on his head. "Hello, sir. Fine day we have here. We're looking to meet a friend."

The boatman hacks up a coughing puff of pipe tobacco smoke and peers back at Pack smugly. "Nobody here but me, 'n I ain't no friend to either of yous, that I kin recall."

~*~

Elliott sits on the riverbank, as her horse grazes nearby. With a stem of grass between her teeth, she watches the short exchange between Pack and the river man. Pack dismounts and walks over to her, letting his horse wander closer to hers. She speaks over her shoulder, as he squats on his haunches. "He ain't here, huh?"

"Nope… He left us a message to meet him south of here, in the next town."

With an apologetic look, Elliott studies her partner as he stares quietly across the flowing river. "Are you thinkin' he might'a run off with it?"

He picks up a piece of driftwood from the grass and pokes it into the soft ground a few times before speaking. "Could be. We'll ask 'im when we find 'im."

"You think he'll still be headed south?"

Pack shrugs his shoulders and tosses the branch away. "I have known Griz a long time, 'nd he's about half-honest. He'll figure to move on south, as planned. We jest have to catch up to him before he crosses that border and spends all the money on some Mexican señorita."

Elliott rubs her eye and smiles at Pack in a sincere, loving way. "You're pretty trusting of your friends."

Pack pats his hands on bended knees and stands upright. "Hey, that's all I've got." He reaches down to give her a hand. "Let's get across this river and keep some distance on whoever might be following. The more trail we get behind us, the better our odds of eluding 'em for good."

She grabs his outstretched hand and pulls herself up. "Hell, maybe they gave up and all just headed back to town."

Amused, Pack gives a slight snort and smiles at her. "Sure they did..."

~*~

With the boat pulled across the river, the hooves of the horses clomp on the wooden planks, as Pack and Elliott lead them off the ferry. The raft lifts higher in the water, as it is relieved of its burden. After thanking the boatman, they mount up and lope their mounts toward the distant hills.

Nodding, the boatman clenches his smoking pipe between his teeth and then slowly tows the ferry back to the opposite shore. He studies the northern horizon and makes out a rising, hazy cloud of dust. He looks to the pair of riders he just let off. "Looks to be a busy day."

~*~

Hank and Fisk ride, side-by-side at a brisk pace. Neither carries the soiled money sacks. As Hank turns to look behind, Fisk studies the path ahead of them and comments. "They're in front of us, not behind us."

"It's a mistake to not always be sure."

Fisk sniffs his fingers and shakes his head, crinkling his nose at the lingering shit-smell from the bank holdup sacks. "Those sneaky sons-a-bitches! Pullin' one on us like that."

Hank grins, as he contemplates on Elliott's attractive features. "She always was distrustin' of a simple plan."

"Think they had it planned that way?"

"Pack is a crafty one alright, but he also has the distinct weakness of being honest."

Fisk shakes his head and sucks at his swelled-up lip. "You know, I never did trust a woman."

Hank looks over at him surprised. "No?"

Fisk nods, serious. "I ain't as dumb as I look."

The comment strikes Hank as humorous, and he reflects back to an old memory. "I did trust one… once."

"Yeah? What happened?"

"She was involved with someone else and was loyal to him."

Fisk waits for more of the story, but nothing comes. "How do you suppose we're gonna to get around that posse and get to the money first?"

Hank replies, "There's a river crossing jest up ahead. We get across, and it's practically a straight run down through Texas for Mexico."

"Hell, everyone is prob'ly on the other side."

Hank looks to Fisk and smiles keenly. "It's not about gettin' to the money first... It's about who ends up with it last." Nodding his agreement, Fisk follows Hank's lead as they move on at a faster trot.

~*~

The cool of evening settles in, as the sun dips below the mountainous horizon to the west. The assembled posse stands at the ferry-crossing blocked-off by the boatman blocking their path to the raft. With his pipe clenched firm between his teeth, he puffs out a grey, wafting cloud of smoke and determinedly shakes his head. The leader stares down at the man and speaks with some urgency. "We need to be on the other side."

"You kin swim it, as much as I care."

"We would prefer the ferry."

"Can't do it."

"Why is that?"

The boatman takes the pipe from between his gritted teeth and spits. "I don't do the crossing at night."

"Why not?"

" A'cause it's dark..."

Noticing the night sky coming on, the frustrated gentleman clenches his jaw and turns to his second-in-command. "We'll rest the horses here until first light, and then we'll continue tracking them across the river."

Stokes looks back at the posse of men and receives a nod of confirmation that they all heard the order. "Yes, sir."

Looking down his nose, the well-dressed gentleman peers at the operator of the ferry. "Suit you okay, sir?"

"Suits me fine, right down to my brogans."

The boatman grins through scattered teeth, as the disgruntled gentleman groans and turns his horse away.

19

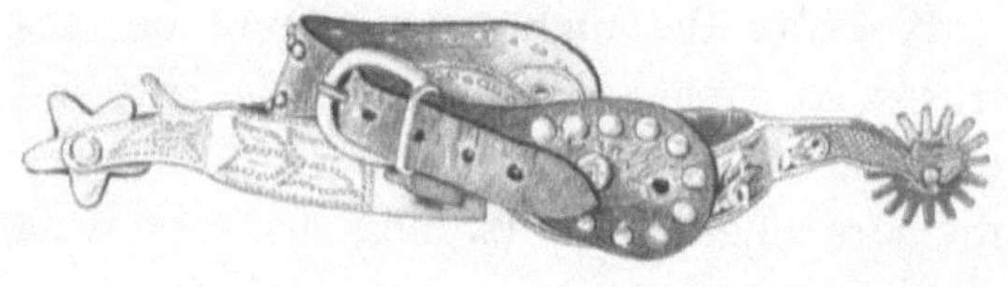

A small campfire lights up the evening sky. Pack and Elliott pass a warmed-up can of beans back and forth between them. Elliott's eyes flicker with longtime affection, as she watches Pack dip his spoon down to scrape the bottom of the can. "Were do you figure we'll catch up with Griz?"

He scoops a spoonful of warm beans into his mouth and passes her the tin can. "I ain't been south this way since I was a kid. Griz is a lot more familiar with the ins and outs."

Elliott twirls the utensil in the soupy remainders at the bottom of the container and scoops up a small portion to eat. "I know a few of 'em."

"You spend time in Texas?"

She passes him the tin with the remainder of the beans. "I was born 'n raised in San Antone."

Pack glances at her and raises an eyebrow before taking the last scoop of their meal. "I didn't know you was a Texan."

"It never come up."

Pack laughs, as he chews, and then swallows. "Heck, most Texans cain't help but make it come up."

"I warn't no southern belle, but I'm surely not a Yankee."

"Got somethin' against northerners?"

"No... Jest saying my blood is in the South."

He shrugs, licks the spoon again and wipes it on his pants leg. "I don't know if Griz will be crossing through your old stomping grounds, but we need to be careful not to pass him by somewhere." He sweeps a curled finger inside the can for the last remaining bean juice, and licks the finger clean. "He knows we'll be following, and he'll be sure to watch out for Hank."

Pack is about to toss the spoon and empty can away, but Elliott leans forward and puts her hand out. "Here… Give me that. I'll clean it proper."

Amused, he hands it over and looks at her. "Why?"

"So we can eat with it again."

"It's just food… It ain't dirty."

Elliott gives Pack a look that makes him feel like a kid. "After wiping it on your britches, it's dirty."

"Better'n your ol' latrine-waders."

She sets the empty bean can by her saddle blanket, opens her canteen before rinsing the spoon, and gazes at him. "You ever been married Pack?"

He looks at her across the firelight and seriously ponders for a moment before replying. "You know, they say a man will never know true happiness until he's been married." Her eyes light up with a hint of promise until he continues, "…And then, it's too late." He laughs, as he holds up his empty hands and pushes back the cuff of his shirt sleeve. "Have you ever seen any shackles holding me down or a branding mark on me?"

She smiles and persists with the inquisition. "No Pack. No hobbles on you that I seen, but you probably lived some sort of a life 'fore we met."

The further inquiry seems to surprise him with her inquisitiveness about his past. "Uh… No, Elliott, I ain't never been married. You?"

"Yeah… Once…"

Hiding his feelings, He puts another stick on the fire. "You never mentioned it."

She raises an eyebrow at him. "You never asked."

They both stare silently into the fire for a moment. Suddenly, Pack gets a dreadful feeling deep down in his gut and looks over at her. "It wasn't Hank, was it?"

Elliott shakes her head. "No, but he knew 'im."

"Where is he now?"

With a far-off gaze, Elliott reflects on her own history as if unloading a weighty burden. "He got killed while I was waiting for him in Fort Worth… It was likely in a card game. The news came to me that he was cashed in and that was that, so I moved north and haven't been back to Texas since."

Pack nods his head and tries to quell the uneasy feeling in his gut. "I'm sorry to hear it."

"Which part?"

"The sad part."

With a contented sigh, Elliott acknowledges that she won't get any sort of deep meaningful emotions out of him. "It will be good to be back on Texas soil."

Pack shrugs. "Looks like any other."

"It ain't."

As the small fire slowly dies down, Pack shifts into his blanket and covers his face with his broad brimmed hat. In the dimming glow of the campfire, Elliott watches him a while. She then curls up under her blanket, as well.

He peeks out from under his hat and grins at her. "Goodnight, Elliott."

"Night, Pack."

20

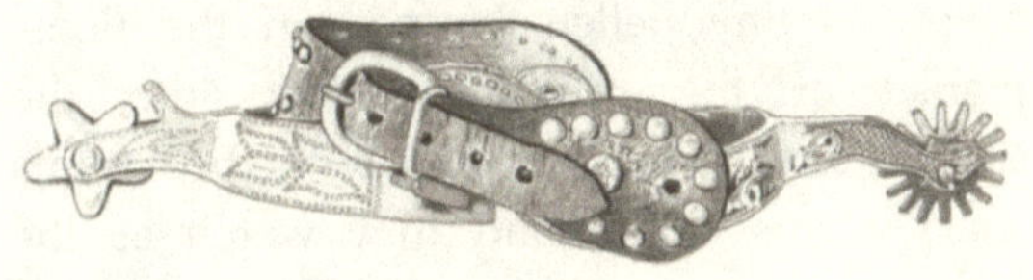

The morning sky is just starting to show a hint of brightness, as a thick, rising mist comes up from the wide, flowing river. The temperature drops several degrees with the break of day. With neckerchiefs tied securely around the horse's muzzles, to keep their mounts quiet, Hank and Fisk step up to the ferry.

Quietly, they climb aboard and Fisk fastens the horses to the railing, while Hank releases the raft's shore tether. Working together, they both tug on the heavy rope that dips down into the current and is secured to the opposite bank. Hank and Fisk move the rope through the rings connecting it to the side rail and the wooden raft eases out into the current. Gripping the rope and working their way down the length of the wooden vessel, the wet line quietly jangles through the holding collars mixing with the sound of shuffling feet.

The morning peace is shattered by the blast of a shotgun. Hank and Fisk both duck for cover, as tiny pellets bounce off the floor-planks of the raft and plink into the surrounding water. The door to the boatman's shack slams closed and they watch as the crusty character reloads the breach of his single-shot bird gun.

Awakened from their camp on the riverbank, several members of the posse rush to the boat dock with their rifles. Hank gives Fisk a shove and grabs ahold of the rope again. "C'mon, Fisk! Keep pulling. We'll be out of gun range soon."

Next to Fisk, a rifle slug splinters away the wood rail. His eyes go wide and he jumps to his feet to resume pulling. Several more fired rounds slap into the wood decking, and the horses begin to kick and stomp in protest. Fisk keeps working at the rope, as Hank jumps to grab the bridles of the animals in an attempt to settle them down.

In front of the shack, the boatman tosses his shotgun to the porch and takes his pipe from his pocket. He packs some tobacco into the clay bowl, as he watches the posse lob bullets over the moving water, just shy of the raft. Striking a match, he lights the tobacco and hollers to them. "Hold yer durn fire, you damned fools!" They glance over at him, and then they continue with their high-aimed shots, that arc though the sky to gain greater distance.

While the boatman smokes his pipe, the leader of the posse walks over to address him. "Who is that on your raft?"

"Hell if I know. They sure as shit didn't pay me!" Several more rounds of lobbed bullets crash into the ferry and the horses lash out and kick sections of the hitching-rail free. The exasperated boat man stomps both his feet and grouses, "If you don't get your men to stop shootin' at my boat, there ain't gonna be nothin' left for you to cross in fer thirty miles!"

They watch as the raft slowly pulls to the middle of the river and the gentleman calls out the order, "Hold your fire!" One more gunshot pops off, and the men lower their rifles to watch the ferry boat slowly make its way to the opposite shore of the river. The mysterious gentleman stares ahead a while then finally looks over at the boatman, standing beside him. "How long will it take for you to bring the vessel back?"

The boatman chokes on a drag from his pipe and hacks a cough. "Uh... I'm jest an old man. Why don't you swim one of your fellas across to bring 'er back?"

The gentleman's fierce gaze pierces right through the boatman. "I will be needing all these men. If you don't survive the swim, then I will send one of them."

The pipe stem drops from the boatman's mouth, with a wisp of smoke, and he gives an affirming nod. From behind, Stokes levers his rifle and gives a soft poke of the gun barrel to the ferry owner's back. "Best start swimming, fella."

They all watch, as the raft reaches the opposite shore, and the two ferry-boat thieves unload their agitated animals. The ferryman dumps the unused tobacco from his pipe and puts it back into his pocket. Reluctantly, he begins to take off the straps to his overalls. "Should take me about an hour."

The gentleman studies the opposite shore and replies. "Make it thirty minutes."

Standing on the riverbank in his dirty, red-faded long-handle underwear, the boatman glances back to the posse leader and then to Stokes, who is still pointing a rifle at him. "That water is pretty cold."

Stokes replies, "Be sure to swim fast."

The boatman makes an obvious gulping sound, as he slips his bare feet into the frigid water. He gives a hesitant shiver before plopping in. Stokes and the posse leader watch as Hank and Fisk mount their horses and wave goodbye before moving down the road. Stokes narrows his eyes and mutters to his boss. "Them two look like the ones from town?"

The gentleman gives a small nod in agreement, as he watches them ride off. "Yes... Yes, they do."

21

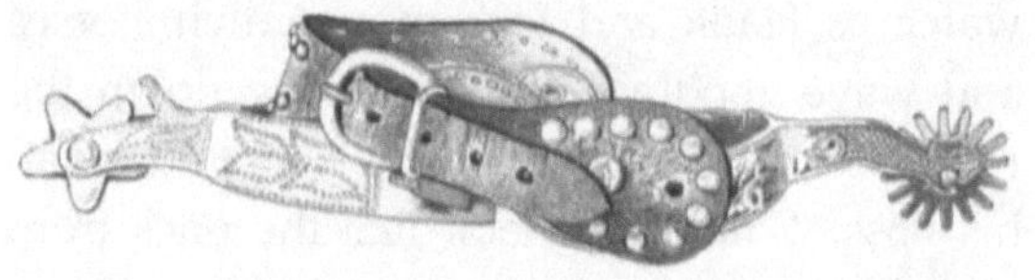

After several days' ride, Pack and Elliott make their way into the Texas panhandle. The wide-open terrain is in stark contrast to the forests, rocks and snow-capped mountains of the north. As they crest a rise, Pack looks behind at what appears to be horseback figures on their trail. "Elliott, do you still have that long-distance glass?"

She halts her mount and looks to Pack curiously. "Yeah... Can you see someone following us?" He nods to her, and she leans back to unfasten the flap on her saddlebag. Elliott pulls out a telescoping spyglass and hands it to Pack. Turning her horse, she leans down on the saddle horn, squints into the distance and waits. "Make out who it is?"

Pack lowers the shiny, brass tube and slides it closed. "No, but I have a good idea."

~*~

A brief shimmer of sunlight reflected off something shiny on the far horizon stops Hank and Fisk in their tracks. They hold-up their horses together and look to one another. Fisk shades his eyes from the mid-day glare as he speaks. "Did you see that, Hank?"

"Yep."

"You think it's them?"

Hank looks around at the flat, barren surroundings. "Who else would be here in this god-forsaken part of Texas?" They urge their horses forward and continue on their way. Not far to the west, concealed by a dip in the terrain, twelve mounted Indians silently watch the pair of southbound riders.

~*~

The posse gallops to an open area where Hank and Fisk had recently rested their mounts. A choking cloud of alkaline dust swirls around them, as the hard-rode group of horses snort for air. The leader looks to the horseman next to him. "How far are they?"

Stokes motions for the tracker to dismount and inspect the ground near a small cluster of rocks. "They can't be far." The buckskin-clad scout has an uneasy look on his face, as he leads his horse back to the group. Stokes looks at the posse and then back down to the scout. "What is it you see?"

"We are close on their trail."

"But?"

"We are not the only ones on this path. Ten, maybe a dozen, unshod ponies are following the ones we are after."

The leader turns to gaze into the near distance, displaying no emotion. Stokes wipes dust from his mouth and spits. "Indians?" The scout nods somberly while studying their vulnerable position, in the open, and the distance to any protective cover. Stokes eases his mount alongside the leader's horse and talks low. "Do you want me to warn the men?"

With a stoic gaze, the gentleman shrugs nonchalantly. "Doesn't matter. If anyone interferes with us, we'll kill them." He looks behind to the posse of armed horsemen and waves them onward.

~*~

Easing down into a ravine, Hank and Fisk ride along, following a faint trail of hoof prints in the sand. A churning cloud of dust travels past them, and a sense of foreboding danger causes the hair on the back of their necks rise. Simultaneously, both riders look up to see the silhouetted figures of leather-fringed riders on the cliff ledge above them. Fisk utters. "Hank…"

"I see 'em."

"Do we talk with them?"

Hank makes a count, taking measure of the odds. "Don't think they're here to talk. Let's jest git!" In swift succession, Hank and Fisk spur their steeds, kicking up dust as they gallop down the ravine.

Following them, the Indians let out a whooping holler, put heel to hide and race in pursuit. The slotted canyon becomes enshrouded in a haze of dust. Some of the warriors lope along the top of the ridge, while others slide their ponies down the steep wall of the ravine and take up the chase.

22

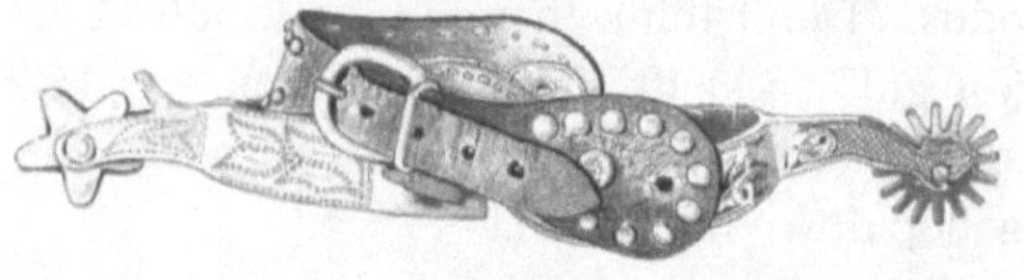

While riding along at a leisurely pace, Pack and Elliott scan the rocky landscape. The sound of the hooves on the dry, dusty ground lulls them into peaceful musings as they travel. Elliott sweeps sweat away from her brow, as she gazes up at the midday sun. "Any thoughts on us findin' Griz?"

Pack lets his horse find its most comfortable walking stride and sits back against the high cantle of his saddle seat. "I guess we'll jest keep on headin' south till there's some sort of civilization. He'll keep movin', unless the temptation to spend some of that money proves to be too much for him."

Elliott's concerned expression shows a kind sympathy for Griz. "It ain't his fault. I swayed him."

He looks over at her and nods. "He is the way he is. There's no fault to be had."

Glancing over her shoulder, Elliott notices a dusty-cloud of haze rising from the ravine they just rode out of. "Uh... Hey there, Pack..."

He shakes his head, as he keeps watching forward. "I've known Griz a long time. Let's not talk about it."

Elliott turns herself in the saddle and points backward. "I think we should talk about this."

He halts his mount and turns in the direction that she points. Taking a gander at what she is referencing, he utters, "Jeez, what is that?"

"Suppose its jest the wind?"

At full tilt, the galloping riders emerge from the ravine. Close behind them, a dozen screaming Comanche warriors ride in hot pursuit. Quickly recognizing that Hank and Fisk are riding for their lives, Pack slaps an open palm to the flank of Elliott's horse and waves her on. "Go... Go!"

Leaping to a gallop, Pack and Elliott take the lead of the two riders and their native pursuers, weaving around scrub brush and boulders. Pack turns his head to peek back at the couple racing behind them and recognizes their desperation. He hollers over to Elliott, as she gallops along beside him. "We're not gonna be able to outrun these Indians."

She calls back to him. "You and your quick thinking would come in real handy 'bout now."

"I'm thinkin' dammit!"

In spite of the impending danger, Elliott can't help but crack a smile. "I guess it's back old Plan-A?"

He keeps the pace by slapping the tail of his reins across the hindquarters of his mount, as he looks aside to her. "Plan-A? What's that?"

"Shoot our way out!" Elliott laughs, and Pack shakes his head with an appearance of disgust while he scans the surrounding terrain for any opportunity of escape.

The hellacious war screams of the pursuing natives ring with a wicked amusement. After a mile of running at an exhausting pace, the horses begin to flag. White foam drips from the corners of their mouths, and lather slides from their haunches like thick slabs of butter.

Pack spots something on the horizon and points. "There! Over there... Head for that flat!!!"

Keeping pace alongside him, Elliott veers her horse in the direction of his gesture. She looks behind at the two fleeing riders and the screaming natives in pursuit. Attempting to follow as best they can, Hank and Fisk whip the last ounce of spirit from their exhausted mounts.

As they crest a rise, they are suddenly faced with what Pack caught a glimpse of earlier. Standing nearly twice the height of a horse, tethered on a long lead-rope tied to a stake, stand two sandy-blond, shaggy-haired camels. The round humps on their backs stand in perfect symmetry with the rocks and boulders of the surrounding landscape.

Raising their long necks from their grazing, slotted nostrils flare as they let out a loud, bleating-bawl of greeting. Wide-eyed panic gives the exhausted horses a second wind of anxious energy. When his horse skids and jolts to a standstill, Fisk is instantly vaulted over the animal's neck to land ungracefully on the rocky ground.

The others hold on tight to their bucking mounts, and Fisk gets up to chase after his skittish horse. In the distance, the Indians halt their pursuit, tentatively observing the two, long-legged animals from a safe distance. The dust settles, as the horseback Indians line up to watch the odd encounter. Then suddenly, they avert their eyes and disperse, promptly disappearing behind the hillside.

Riding out a fit of bucking, Pack regains control of his mount and steers it timidly toward the pair of camels. Approaching desert creatures, Pack notices something fastened to the stake that secures the animals. He reaches down and tears away the fluttering paper. Holding the note, he reads a scribbled message:

You gonna need these - G.

Pack smiles, as he scans the barren terrain that surrounds him. He notices Hank giving a wide berth to the camels he is curiously circling, and that the two animals bob their heads in unison as they gaze back at him. He turns to look at Elliott as she rides up and queries, "What's it say?"

"Griz sends his best."

23

Surrounded by the desolate Texas landscape, Pack and Elliott sort through their saddle gear, trying to figure out how to load their things on the camels, while Hank paces around them. Pausing in his stride, he looks to the west and sees Fisk returning without a horse. Hank looks at the pair near the camels and grumbles, "You can't be serious... That crafty old codger has got all that stolen money with him?"

Pack looks up from the pile of saddle tack and shrugs. "As far as we know."

Hank watches Elliott unfasten leather rigging from her saddle to use on the camel setup. Unsure, he shakes his head, looks at the pair of long-legged desert creatures and grunts, "You really think that is a good idea, sweetheart?"

"If Griz says this is the way, then that's what we do."

Baffled, Hank replies. "All the way to Mexico?"

"Why not?"

"Why did you give that old fool all the coin?"

Elliott turns to face Hank and gives him the stink-eye. "You and Fisk couldn't steal from us what you couldn't find."

"But, we had a deal!"

Pack considers how to saddle an animal with a hump. He glances over to Fisk, walking over, and replies to Hank. "Were you really gonna return the money?"

"No, prob'ly not."

Elliott gives Hank a knowing look and continues to unlace the securing leather straps from under her saddle. Unsatisfied with the progress of their pithy conversation, Hank looks away from her to watch his partner's approach. His attention is distracted by Pack's efforts to coax one of the camels down to its padded knees. He shakes his head in disbelief.

"Pack, I don't know if you consider this some kind of a joke, but I'm not ridin' that thing."

After getting the animal to bend down to settle on the ground, Pack examines it in terms of saddle–rigging options. "Suit yerself. Our horses are all broke down and won't last another day without water." Pack smoothes his hand over the curved back of the camel.

Hank eyes the creature with distaste. "Heck, Pack. What do you know about this thing?"

Pack gestures to the *U.S.* branding on the camel's flank. "I know these are genuine United States Government service camels, and they're suited for this dry, rocky terrain."

"How'd Griz get a hold of 'em?"

"Don't care. Borrowed 'em, bought 'em or found 'em. They're prob'ly one of Beale's surplus animals that got released to the wild after the war."

They both turn as Fisk drags his tired feet toward them, until finally sitting himself on the ground, exhausted. Then, the camel belches and hocks an arching wad of spittle a few feet away from the cowboy. Pack shrugs. "Probably jest like ridin' a horse, 'cept bigger."

Hank shakes his head. "I ain't doing it…"

"Well, suit yerself."

"That thing ain't fit to ride on!" In the background, Hank's horse, still under saddle and sweated-up with cakes of lather, lets out a coughing groan while swaying at the knees. Slowly it lowers itself to the ground, flops over on its side and kicks out its legs. Mournfully, they all watch as the horse breathes its last. Hank and Pack exchange a look of regret. "Well... They smell god-awful." The standing camel puckers its lips and spits a wad of saliva at Hank, hitting him with some of the spray. He shakes his head, as he wipes the spittle off his shoulder. "Horses don't do that!"

Pack lifts one of the saddles from the ground and tries to fit it over the hump of the kneeling camel. "Like I said... Suit yerself."

Hank looks to Fisk for support, but the seated cowboy only shakes his head, kicks out his boot heels out and murmurs, "Sure beats walkin'."

~*~

Pack and Elliott cross the wide-open, desert terrain atop a slow-moving camel. Seated in front, Pack attempts to steer using the two sets of leather reins, fastened together, in order to breech the long distance between head and hump. They seem relatively comfortable astride the makeshift rig, with

Elliott clinging to him as they sway in unison to the lanky gait of the tall animal.

Close behind, Hank coaxes his camel along, as Fisk awkwardly tries to find a place to grip his feet and hold on. He winces and grips tighter with every step the camel takes. "Remember what I said about walkin'? Well, I take it back!"

Hank adjusts his awkward position on the camel's hump and writhes at Fisk's tightening grip. "Dammit Fisk! Then, git off!" Hank tries to push Fisk's groping hands away. "You're clutchin' and grabbin' at me like a lonely prospector at a peep show. Yer jest makin' it worse all the durn time."

"This warn't my damned idea to come down to God-awful Texas and see if we can ride some furry dinosaur."

Hank tries to peel off the desperate grip, but Fisk clutches tighter. "If you don't want your cut of the money, then let go of me and get off."

Fisk shimmies his boots against the camel's sides and tries to keep from slipping down the back of the sloped hump. "Heck, that old coot prob'ly drank all the money up already, or pissed it away with some crooked-toothed whore."

Hank reaches down to push at Fisk's embracing hold around his waist. He looks back to his partner and growls, "I'll kill 'im if he has."

Scrambling his boot heels on the camel's flank again, Fisk tries to gain some sort of steady hold on the furry hide. He continues griping to his partner, as he starts to slip down the animal's rump. "We should have killed him before."

Hank turns around and pulls Fisk back up to a secure position. "Yeah... Maybe so."

24

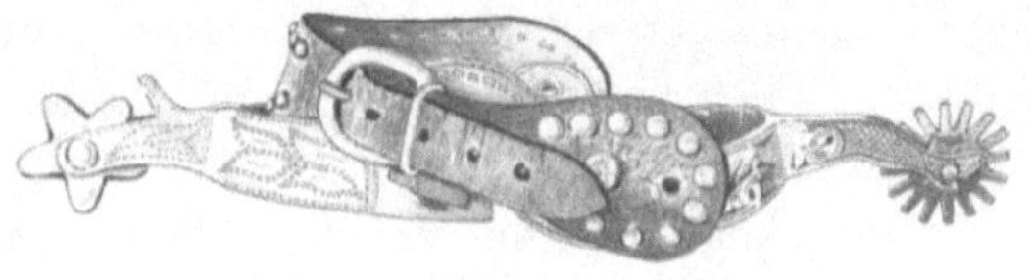

Like a passage from *The Arabian Nights*, the pairs of unlikely companions sit around a campfire. The camels stand behind, exotically illuminated by the firelight. Favoring his tailbone, Hank lies on his side to ease the discomfort. He rubs his soreness, with a groan, and Elliott smiles at him remarking. "You got hump-rump there, Hank?"

Pack laughs with amusement, as he lights up a smoke. Hank shoots an annoyed glance Pack's way and murmurs. "Very funny. I'm not sure who I'm angrier with… you or her." Hank hooks a thumb past his shoulder at Fisk sitting cross-legged by the fire. "Tomorrow,

I'll ride with Elliott, and you can have him pawin' at you like a horny mountain-cat."

Looking up from the campfire, Fisk makes a sour face. "Piss on you, Hank. It warn't no more comfortable behind the hump than on top. I got this awful animal smell on me, and I'm sore all over from jest hangin' on."

A puff of smoke blows out from Pack's mouth as he exhales a drag from his lit tobacco. "I'll help ya set up a better saddle-riggin' tomorrow."

Elliott jokes across the campfire. "I enjoyed the ride."

Hank notices her gazing fondly at Pack and understands her insinuation. "Yeah... I'll bet you did."

Uncomfortable with being teased in front of the others, Pack ignores the comment and takes another drag of his cigarette. "We should only need 'em a few more days, till we get nearer to Fort Clark."

Hank settles along his hip, avoiding his raw backside. "Is that where our pal Griz is waiting?"

Pack shrugs in reply. "Don't know, guess he could be."

Dismayed, Hank looks back and forth, from Pack to Elliott. "Heck of a way to run a partnership... Didn't you tell the 'ol codger where to meet with the money?"

Pack looks over to Elliott and gives her a knowing look. "The idea has been something of a mystery from the get-go."

She winks at him, tips her hat over her eyes and lies back against her saddle. "Ain't that always the way with men? You make a plan, and then go on and do your own thing."

Pack, trying to decipher her cryptic statement, looks skeptical at her. He takes a final puff from his rolled smoke, and tosses the stub into the fire. "Ya never told me of a plan."

"The hell I haven't."

"When?"

"From the first day we met." She covers a sweet smile with her hat and pulls up her blanket. "Nighty-night, Pack."

Pack looks at Fisk settling under his saddle-blanket, and then over to where Hank lies uncomfortably on his side. "She never told me of any particulars since she found it."

Hank snorts, as he uses a poker stick on the fire. "Don't ask us to explain it. She's your partner."

~*~

Trotting along at a steady gait, the two camels pack their loads with the ease of an animal suited to the terrain. They are surrounded by a vast western landscape of scrub brush, sandy rock formations, and cactus bloom. At the top of the hump of one camel, Elliott slips her hand around Pack's waist and unties her canteen from the jury-rigged saddle. "This is kind of fun. The circus came to Fort Worth once, and they had camels to ride."

Pack feels her tight grip around his middle and glances back over his shoulder. "It loses its charm after a day or so."

She takes a swallow from the canteen and smiles. "Aww, I like the change in the norm to shake things up."

"Well, you diving into the crapper sure put a change-up into our norm..."

She fastens the canteen on the saddle-rigging again, snugs her pelvis closer to Pack's backside and whispers softly, "You regret hitchin' up with me?"

He mulls over her odd choice of wording and replies, "You've been a good partner... As good as Griz, at least." Elliott rolls her eyes and puts her chin over Pack's shoulder. "Suppose Griz will have it pretty-well spent by now?"

"There's a good chance of it. I've never known him to hang on to extra coin for long."

As she speaks, her breath on his ear sends gooseflesh up his arm. "Hmm… At his age, he deserves a good hurrah."

"At his age, he's had more than his share of fun."

"Ladies don't flock around like they once did."

Pack turns his head to face Elliott. "With that much money on him, he won't have any trouble attracting female attentions." For an instant, his eyes connect with hers and he pivots forward. "If he blows it on whiskey, women and cards, this'll all be for nothin'!"

"Not really… He'll have had the time of his life, and we'll have a clear shot at Mexico."

Pack glances back at her again. "This ain't some trick to get me to Mexico, is it?"   She puts on an innocent smile and rests her chin back on his shoulder. "Would I con you?"

Pack ponders a moment, looks over to Hank and Fisk, embraced uncomfortably on the big hump of the other camel, and then he turns back forward. After a while, he responds. "You better not be."

"Like you're always sayin'… *no one can make you do something' you don't already want to do.*"

"Don't go and be using my own words 'gainst me."

Elliott sits back, grinning. "I was just remindin' you of your own insightful wisdom."

"Let's talk about something else."

"Like what?" She stretches her spine and looks back to watch the unfortunate pair riding double on the other plodding camel. Suddenly, on the horizon, she begins to make out the forms of a large group of horsemen. "Pack?"

"Yeah?"

"Do you think those Injuns would come back around?"

She reaches behind to her saddlebags and starts to unbuckle one of the cover flaps, as Pack casually responds. "They're more afraid of these beasts than the horses were."

Maneuvering to the rear of the saddle-rig, trying not to slip off, Elliott pulls out her spyglass and extends the eyepiece. She aims it at the horizon and focuses it on the posse. Slowly she pans the distance glass along the lineup of riders and pauses on the mysterious gentleman at the center.

"Uh, Pack..."

"Yeah, Elliott?"

"Do you think a posse would follow us this far?"

"I dunno... I guess, if the reward was right."

Glancing at Hank and Fisk and seeing that they haven't noticed yet, Elliott nudges Pack. "How big of a reward?"

"A whole lot more than a hundred bucks."

Reaching around, Elliott passes Pack the extended spyglass and gestures backwards to the horizon as he turns. "Take a look at that ridge..."

25

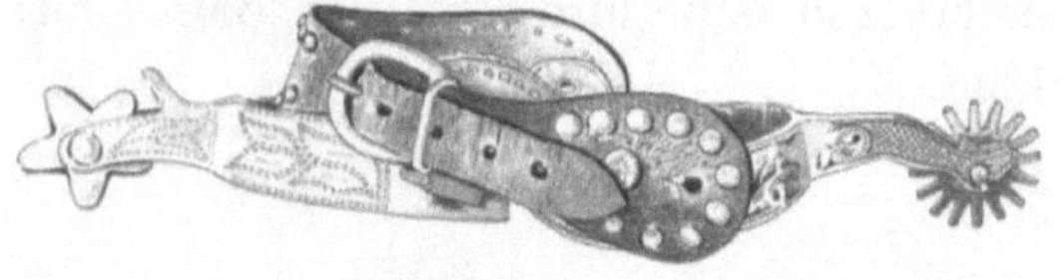

Lined up along the ridge, above the sparse desert landscape, the posse of bounty hunters stands resting their horses. Positioned at the middle of the group, the leader holds a pair of binoculars up to his face, studying the riders to the south. Adjusting the focus, he discerns two men on the back of a camel and then directs his focus to the pair on the back of another camel in the lead.

The gentleman is surprised by a flash of light reflected back at him. He watches as the foremost figure on the camel turns a spyglass in his direction. Through the eyepieces, the two each momentarily examines the other.

~*~

"Oh, shit…"

Already knowing the answer, she inquires, "Uh, Pack. Is it that same posse?"

Pack nods, as he compresses the spyglass. He looks over to the other camel and waves an arm in the direction of the horsemen gathered on the ridge. Hank gives his camel a few awkward kicks and trots up closer to Pack and Elliott. "Damn this long-legged animal! What is it?"

"We've got some admirers."

Hank and Fisk both turn and squint to the horizon. "Suppose them are Injuns?"

"Nope. Looks to be that posse from up north."

"Aww, damn… Really?"

"Appears to be."

Hank curses under his breath and turns back to Pack with a pistol raised. "Warn't sure if they would make it this far, but, since they did, I have to switch sides again."

Elliott glowers at Hank, who merely winks in return. She grumbles, "You haven't changed, you two-faced skunk."

He shrugs, as he glances over his shoulder at the riders racing down from ridge. "Why would I change?" Hank has his gun pointed directly at Pack, while he smirks at Elliott. "Ya see, I happen to like who I am."

While Hank is momentarily distracted, Pack looks around to assess the dire situation. Hank wags the barrel of the pistol at him and warns, "Pack, I've known ya a good while. Don't make me shoot you."

A gunshot rings out in the distance and, close by, a puff of sand rises up from the ground. Unaffected by the sound, the camels continue to walk, as the bullet skitters harmlessly away. Pack turns in the saddle to face the posse that is firing at them. "I won't be the only one who might get shot. They think we have the money."

Several more bullet-strikes kick-up the dirt around them, and Hank lowers his pistol slightly as he turns to look. "No reason to shoot us if we give up the whereabouts of the money and don't run...!"

Pack pushes his camel on, and Hank tries to keep up. "Damn Hank, they don't have a reason not to!"

Fisk holds onto Hank, as he looks back at the galloping horsemen. Wisps of smoke betray the nearly soundless shots being fired from a distance. With an abrupt grunt of agony, Fisk arches his back and slides down the rear of the camel. "Those bastards..."

Hank reaches his free hand back to grab his partner, but misses, as Fisk drops to the ground. "What is it?"   "Goddammit, pard...! I'm shot."

Hank turns to the pair on the other camel and raises his pistol at them again. "This don't change nothin'. Stay put and stop that damned camel!"

Elliott holds tighter onto Pack, as she looks from Hank to the riders quickly gaining on them. "Hank, you're an idiot to think they're gonna spare you."

As shots continue to whiz past them, one hits the leather saddle skirting very close to Hank's leg. Immediately, Hank utters, "What the hell...?" He raises his arms high and waves in surrender toward the quickly approaching posse. "We surrender!"

Bullet lead continues to zing past them, kicking up puffs of dirt well beyond their path. Jumping with a sting to her leg, Elliott clutches her calf. "Aww, shit...!"

Pack turns from looking at Fisk, struggling to keep up, holding his wound, to look at where Elliott clutches her boot. "Where you hit? Did it go through?"

She frowns, as she tries to shake the pain out of her leg, "I think it just glanced off my boot. Hurts like the dickens."

Pack points to Hank sitting turned in the saddle, waving both his arms in the air in a fruitless attempt at peaceful surrender. "Still want to stick around?"

Elliott shakes her head and grimaces. "Hell, no!"

Hank continues to wave his pistol overhead and yells, "Why won't they stop shooting at us?"

Pack grips one of Elliott's arms tighter around his mid- section and gives the camel's flank an urging swat of the reins. "You stick around and ask 'em, Hank."

Hank continues to wave one arm in the air, while aiming his pistol at them as they trot away. "Stop that camel." He looks behind at Fisk who staggers along in a feeble attempt to keep up with the long-legged beasts. "Hold up I said..." Hank takes a shot that whizzes over their heads. "Pack... Elliott, stop dammit!"

Leaving Hank and Fisk behind in the dust, Elliott glances over her shoulder with remorse. Kicking his heels, Pack urges their camel into a stretched-out, loping gallop. Both riders hold tightly to the hump, as the gangly camel leaps through the air on broad, wide-spreading toes.

Hank holsters his pistol, as rifle shots from the approaching horsemen continue to fire off in their direction. He looks down to see his partner doubled over in agony. "Pard, can you climb yerself back up here?" With a pained look, Fisk clutches at the bleeding wound to his torso and shakes his head negatively.

Several bullets thump into the thick hide of the camel, causing it to bellow loudly and step up its rambling stride. Hank fails to slow the trotting animal, and Fisk is gradually left behind. "Sorry pal… Gotta go."

"Hank… Don't leave me…"

Glancing back to the posse, Hank makes up his mind, as he gives the camel an urging kick. The camel canters away and eases into a lope. Fisk stumbles and falls to his knees, calling out, "Hank… you son of a bitch!" He lifts his clenched fist in the air. "I'll kill you for this!"

Without looking back, Hank whips the tail end of the reins against the animal's flank and urges it into a flat-out run.

26

The ungainly camel races through the desert scrub on wide, padded-feet and long, thin legs. Perched on the hump, Pack and Elliott cling tightly to each other as the animal stretches its stride to quicken its running pace. Elliott pushes her chin over his shoulder. "How long can this thing run like this?"

"I surely don't know... Hopefully, a bit longer than those horses in the posse coming after us..."

Glancing behind, Elliott notices Hank whipping his camel to a faster run and coming up on her flank. As their own loaded camel begins to slow down, his, with only the single rider to carry, eventually moves up alongside them. Running abreast of each other, Pack looks over to the lone rider next to him.

Noticing that Fisk is missing, Pack swivels in the saddle to look back. The pursuing horsemen quickly overcome Fisk, racing past without interruption to the chase. Elliott gives Pack's middle a squeeze and points ahead past his shoulder. "Look! There's some cover there... Maybe even water."

In the distance, the distinct green color of vegetation stands out at the base of a cluster of rocks. Pack turns forward, nods, and gives the camel an urging kick with his spur-heels. As the camel steers toward the oasis, Elliott takes off her hat to further motivate the camel with a swat to its hindquarters.

Hank watches Pack and Elliott unexpectedly veer off. He looks back to where Fisk was overrun, and when he turns back, he spots the watering hole on the horizon. Slapping the leather reins and swatting his camel's hindquarters, Hank attempts to keep up the pace, as he follows after the others.

~*~

First to reach the rocks, Hank grabs his rifle and cocks the lever as he leaps from the hump of his camel. Elliott slides down the back of her camel, as Pack steers the trotting animal to the cover of some brush. At the base of the boulders, through the thick vegetation, a small trickle of water seeps from the ground to form a muddy pool. Pack climbs off the animal, as it lowers its head to drink. With flapping lips, the camel slurps from the shallow puddle at the base of the rock. The water level drops, and the slow trickle from the spring struggles to replenish the volume of water lost to the camel's thirst. Pack and Elliott exchange a look of trepidation, as the posse approaches and Pack draws his rifle from its scabbard.

Elliott waves to Hank, as the other camel smells the water and abruptly drifts in their direction. "Back here, Hank! We got some water!"

Hank follows on foot, as his camel lumbers through the brush. With a rifle in one hand, he reaches up to his saddle rig with the other. "Is there water for our canteens?" He looks down at the trickling spring and is shocked to see the camel drain the puddle completely. "Get that furry beast out of there, or he'll suck it dry!"

Turning his attention from the oncoming horsemen, Pack shakes his head in reply, "Letting these animals fill up is the only chance we've got."

Elliott nods in agreement, as she takes hold of the other camel's bridle and leads it to the edge of the watering hole. "There isn't enough here for all their horses to drink at once, so it will slow them up..."

Hank looks to the steadily approaching posse. He turns to see Pack pull his animal away from the water hole to make room for the other camel to drink. "I can hold 'em off here, while you two head south."

Tightening up the saddle cinch on his camel, Pack looks at Hank warily and Elliott voices her skepticism. "And, just why would you do that?"

Nestling into a good shooting position that covers most angles of approach, Hank looks up at Pack and then to Elliott. "Yer askin' too many questions, darlin'... Stop bein' such a girl about it and accept the good fortune handed to you." Hank turns back to Pack and smiles. "Do you have a problem with my staying?"

Pack patiently urges the camel down on its knees, throws a leg over it and jumps into the rigged-up saddle seat. "Nope."

As Pack reaches out his hand to help Elliott climb aboard, she looks at him a moment, and then over to Hank. "Come with us, Hank...

We can make it. Their horses will play out before they catch us."

Pack tilts his chin contrarily. "Actually, they won't... Their horses will drop eventually, but they'll overtake us first. "

Keeping low, Hank puts his rifle to his shoulder and nods his agreement. "Pack is right. Go on and get out of here." He motions them away and smiles. "Say hello to Griz for me, if you ever catch up to him."

As the sound of the galloping posse draws nearer, Elliott sees Hank direct his aim. She grabs Pack's hand and he pulls her up onto the hump of the camel. The beast bellows, as it rises from its knees to its feet. Sitting at the peak of the curved back, Pack turns the camel to Hank and peers down kindly at him. "See ya, Hank."

Hank waves briefly over his shoulder. "Yeah, see ya." The camel's neck cranes around to turn and face southward. Pack kicks the camel into a lope, and they ride away to the sound of gunshots ricocheting off the rock face.

27

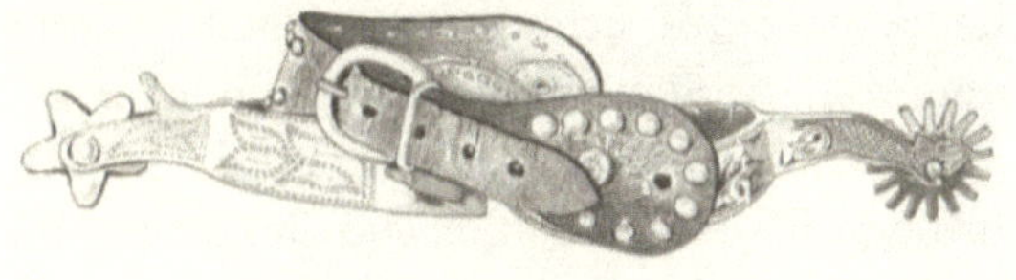

In his tall-shafted, leather riding boots, Pack kicks up dust as he walks through the scrubby brush. He leads the long-legged camel with Elliott perched atop the hump, like a western-attired Queen of Sheba. Just as the outline of Fort Clark's buildings can be seen on the horizon, Pack stops to ease the pain in his feet caused by the slope-heeled cowboy boots. "These shit-kickers ain't made for walkin'."

Elliott wears her long bandana tucked under the brim of her hat to shade her neck and pushes it back in the breeze. "Come back up here with me." She sits, Indian-style, in the saddle and scoots herself back to make room for him.

He looks up to her and shakes his head. "Sittin' up there gets to be like ridin' the mast of a tall ship."

"What do you know about sailing?"

He clears off of patch of ground, takes a seat, kicks off one of his leather boots and rubs the arch of his aching foot. "Hell, I been around the horn when I was jest a youngster."

From high above, Elliott watches Pack massage his stocking foot and imagines him working a sail vessel as a kid. "You was a sailor, huh?"

While he tugs at his sock, he smiles and looks up at her. "Sailors and cowboys got a lot in common as far as lifestyles. It's either workin' with an ocean of water or a sea of cattle."

"Sure… I guess you could see it that way."

"And, there's no money to be made in either."

She laughs and watches him pull off his remaining boot to do the same with his other foot. "You sure do seem to stick with those sorts of occupations."

He peers up at her with a serious expression before breaking into a smile. "Yeah. That's the way it's been so far." Pack pulls on one of his boots and gazes toward Fort Clark. "Well, if Griz is still in the States, this is where he'd be."

Unsure, Elliott replies, "He'll be there."

The camel suddenly bellows a deep groan and bends at the knees, lowering itself to the ground. Elliott holds tight to keep from sliding either forward or backward as it tilts to a kneeling position. She looks at Pack thoughtfully. "I guess he wants you to ride into town in style."

Pack pulls on his other boot and stands before them. "Why the hell not?" Looking at the unsightly animal, he can't help but get the impression that the camel is smiling at him. "First thing we're doin' in town is trading him at the first mission church or livery manger I see, and gettin' something lower to the ground." The smiling camel lets out a throaty belch that displays its funky set of lower teeth and upper gums. It then puckers its meaty lips to spit. Pack leaps aside, avoiding the stream of sputum, and he makes his way around the furry animal to get in position to mount. "The only safe place around this thing is on it."

Elliott smiles at him while reaching out a hand to welcome him up. "Climb aboard, sailor."

~*~

Townspeople greet Pack and Elliott with odd stares and strange, questioning looks as they ride the camel into the provisional settlement built beside the military fort. A hitched team of horses starts to snort and shy aside in the road, as the long-legged beast approaches. The wagon driver tries to keep control over the frightened animals, but they kick at the traces and veer off to the boardwalk. As the camel passes, a wheel gets hung up on one of the building's vertical porch supports.

The driver shakes a fistful of reins at the two riders perched atop the camel, as he hollers from the crashed wagon. "Piss on yer hide, you mangy dog-meat! Get that flea-bitten critter away from the street, you son of a damn mule-lick..."

Pack glances over his shoulder to Elliott and grimaces. "Cover your ears, darlin'... He's jest gettin' warmed-up."

The wagon driver tries to back his team off the boardwalk to free the stuck wheel from the porch rail. Instead, the team turns white eyeballs to the camel ambling in the street and bolts forward. The wooden porch support tears free and the wheel cants to the side, broken at the hub. Continuing his stream of curses, the seething driver hops off the wagon bench and hollers, "You damned dirty jackanapes! If I find you this day, I'll…"

Eager to be rid of the camel, Pack steers the gangly beast toward the nearest saloon. Elliott regards the wagon wreck behind them and whispers over Pack's shoulder, "Maybe we should hide him around back."

"This animal might be a harder trade than I thought." He steers the camel into an alleyway between two wood-framed buildings and their knees nearly scrape the plank wallboards on either side.

Seated high on the camel's back, Elliott notices their wavering reflection in a dark glass window that must have been put in before the other building. She looks inside to see a familiar face in the crowd, seated at a table, playing cards. "Pack… I think I just seen Griz."

Pack turns to look behind at the tunnel-like alleyway. "Where is he?"

"Inside this here building." She puts her hand out to pat the wood siding beyond the window they had just passed. They continue around to the rear of the building, moving under an upper level, rear porch and Pack reaches out to climb onto the railing. Elliott takes up the camel's reins, as Pack swings a leg up over onto the deck of the balcony. "Where are you going?"

"I'll grab Griz and meet you out back." He waves to her, as he locates an open window and dives inside.

28

The saddled camel stands in the back alley, tied off on the support to the upper landing where Pack had dismounted. Elliott stands alongside the tall creature, leans against its flank and takes off her hat. She runs her fingers through her matted hair, trying to fluff some life into the greasy mop.

When the back door to the building opens, she looks up to see Pack step to the porch, alone. "Well…? Was it him?"

Disappointed, he shrugs. "I dunno. Didn't see him anywhere inside… Are you sure?"

"It was a quick look in passing… Maybe it wasn't him." Elliott puts her cowboy hat back on and gazes down the alley. "Do you think he's still here in town?"

Pack tilts his head to the rear entryway of the saloon. "Could be. Let's get a drink and think on it."

As Pack turns to go back inside the building, Griz appears in the open doorway. They stare at each other, speechless for a moment, until Elliott sees him and exclaims, "Griz, You found us!"

Griz breaks his stare with Pack and looks to Elliott. "Uhh, yeah… And, you sure are some hard ones to locate."

Pack grunts, as he turns to see Elliott climb the first step of the porch stairs. "How hard were you looking?"

Eyeballing Griz, Pack notices that he is dressed in his same, nearly-used-up, ragged clothing and old, floppy hat. Elliott rushes up the stairs and pushes past Pack to give Griz an affectionate hug. "How are you? Is it still safe?"

Griz smiles at Elliott through his long whiskers and squeezes her tight. "You know it is, girly."

Pack stands behind the two on the porch and snorts, "He didn't spend any of it on a new set of clothes, at least." The old man runs his fingers through his beard, eye level with the camel hitched on the porch railing. "I see you got my gift. Where's the other one? Ya have ta eat 'im?"

Bewildered, Pack responds, "Camel steaks were not on our menu." He looks at the saloon's back-alley exit and lifts a suspicious eyebrow. "Why were you headed out the back?"

"Huh? No reason in particular."

Elliott grabs Griz by the arm and leads him back through the open doorway. "Doesn't matter now, anyhow. We found you, and all the good times are ahead of us."

Pack watches them disappear inside the saloon door. He thinks a moment, and then has an uneasy feeling as he takes a look down the alleyway. The camel grunts, and Pack glance back at it, before following the others inside.

~*~

Reunited, they sit around a small table in the back corner of the saloon. Pack seems unusually melancholy as Elliott beams at Griz. She pats his craggy hand and whispers. "It sure is wonderful to hear all your old stories again Griz, but where did you put the money?"

The old-timer carefully eyes the room for potential listeners, then leans in closer on the table and waves them in. They each bend a bit forward to hear Griz mutter quietly, "Don't you worry none. It's safe."

Pack puts his elbows to the table and whispers back. "Where exactly is it?"

Griz turns to look at Elliott, when she curiously asks, "Did you hide it somewhere close-by?"

"Kinda…"

Pack looks around the empty saloon, following the old man's gaze as it wanders to the front entry. "You know that stolen money has put us in a lot of trouble… Folks are chasing us and ready to kill for it." Thinking back to their last encounter with Hank and Fisk, Pack continues. "Some may have been killed already."

Griz scratches his beard, nodding and Elliott chimes in. "We knew it would be safe with you. Is it with your stuff?"

"No. That wouldn't be too safe."

From the uneasy look on Griz's face, Pack gets an uncomfortable feeling. "Where in town is it, Griz?"

"Well, ya see… It's not here in town anymore."

Pack groans, "You don't have it here?"

"Not exactly…"

Eyes wide with disbelief, Elliott exclaims, "What?!?"

In a huff, Pack sits back against his chair and grumbles, "Dammit! Where is it then?"

Griz gestures them in to the middle of the table again, and they all lean closer, as the old-timer hoarsely whispers, "Ya see, I gave it to a friend of mine."

Elliott gapes, waiting for a punch line, before replying, "You're kidding… Right?"

Pack shakes his head and grimaces at Elliott. "Damn, I knew it. We risked our necks, and it's gone."

Puzzled, Griz looks at them and wobbles his jaw. "Naw, its fine… He doesn't even know he has it."

Reclining in his chair, Pack tips his hat back on his head. "I won't even ask why, because the things that go through either of your minds are beyond me." He adjusts his hat forward again and looks directly at Griz. "Where can we find this friend of yours?"

Cracking a beaming smile through his coarse whiskers, Griz motions them in again and speaks with a lowered tone. "Ya see… I figured it was way too dangerous for me to carry that much stolen dinero across the Mexican border by myself, so I slipped it into my pal's town supplies. He works for the federal government, surveilling the southern border against attacks from Poncho Villa and his sorts."

Pack exchanges a bewildered look with Elliott and turns to Griz. "So, he's down along the border somewhere?"

"Prit' near."

"How far?"

Griz smiles, seemingly very impressed with himself. "South of Laredo a spell. Nearer to the crossing at Los Saenz and San Pedro de Roma."

Elliott puts on a smile and shrugs her reluctant consent. "It's not the worst idea you've ever had."

Pack shoots her a troubled look and turns back to Griz. "You hold on to any of that money?"

"Jest a smidgen to get by on…"

"Good thing. We need to acquire some mounts, get resupplied and rid ourselves of that smelly camel."

Elliott nods and sniffs along her coat sleeve and hand. "I would like to have a bath."

Griz grins wider and rubs his hand across his nose. "You both is starting to smell like that knobby-kneed critter. Noticed it right off."

Taking a quick sniff of himself, Pack shakes his head. "When you advise us on hygiene, it's a sad day."

The old-timer hooks his thumb over his shoulder to the main street. "There is a bath house a few doors down 'nd a livery stable at the edge of town. If'n you want a special treat, you kin have a tub brought up to my room."

Elliott looks at Griz and around the saloon interior. "You have a room here?"

"What good is money, if'n you don't spend it?"

Pack rolls his eyes and glances to the upstairs level. "Depends on whose money it is, I guess…"

Surprised, they both look over at Pack. Elliott snorts at him sarcastically. "You should be the one to talk about using other folk's money!"

At a loss for words, Pack stares at her, until Griz smooths his hand across the table. "Now that we're reunited, what do you want to do first?"

Elliott looks at the stairway leading the rooms above. "How about a bath first?"

Griz thumps his fingers on the table and nods. "Mine is room number seven. I'll have a tub sent up."

Pack glances to the street outside and then back again. "Go ahead and do that." He looks toward Griz, then to Elliott. "We'll unload that durned camel and get some new mounts. When we're resupplied, we'll meet you back here."

29

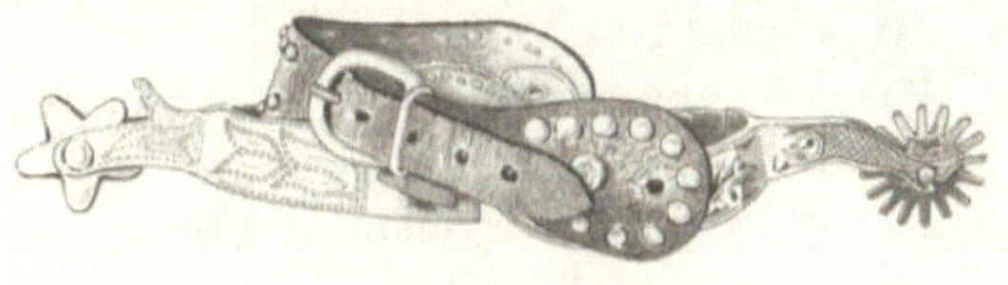

A copper bathing tub sits near windowed balcony doors in the largest room of the hotel. Soaking in the sudsy water, Elliott lays her head back on the rim of the tub and pokes a foot out over the other end. She splashes the cloudy water and leisurely washes her body beneath the soap-filmed surface. The sound of horses, wagons and daytime business clamors up from street, and she dunks her head under the water while raising a bare leg into the air.

~*~

The camel stands at the stockade fence near the livery barn with his head held high over a herd of longhorn cattle. Pack works at saddling a horse and Griz comes over with another horse and gear. The old-timer watches his partner, and Pack grins then tilts his head aside toward the lone camel. "I was surprised to get even ten dollars for him."

Griz gives a grunt, as he tosses a saddle over his blanketed mounts. "Bit more'n I paid for 'em."

"Where did you get the pair?"

Reaching under the belly of his horse, Griz grabs the cinch strap and loops it through the ring on the other side. "Swapped with an old, Indian horse-trader I know, who said they was needed to cross that dry terrain."

Pack continues the job of saddling then pauses to think. "Dang, I thought Injuns were scared to death of them things?"

"Most of 'em are. This one's a loner that cain't afford to be afraid and pass on a good deal." They both resume the task at hand. Pack moves around one of the horses and stands next to Griz to inspect the rig. With a smile, he looks over at his old friend and nods his head. "I warn't sure we'd find you."

Griz peers back over his shoulder to Pack. "Yeah?"

"You think any about not being found?"

Pausing, Griz shrugs. "You found me, didn't ya?"

"Yup... No use thinkin' on what could've been."

The old man grins, and winks at his longtime partner. "Besides, I don't even have the money, remember?"

Pack frowns in reply. "Oh yeah, you always did claim *Lack of temptation leads to virtue.*"

Griz chuckles and pats the leather seat of his saddle. "Amen, brother."

Using the lower railing of the corral fence, Griz gets a step up and swings his leg over to settle into the saddle seat. He looks down at Pack, tying the securing straps on a pair of saddle bags. "You tell that girl what you think of her yet?"

"Who?"

"Elliott, ya durned fool..."

Pack looks confused, as he finishes with the leather ties. "What do you mean?" Griz grumbles something gruff and unintelligible, and Pack asks him again. "Tell her what?"

"Don't you know?"

"What should I tell her?"

"Guess not..."

Hopping his foot onto the stirrup, Pack steps up, swings a leg over and mounts. "What in the heck are you mumblin' about, old man?"

Griz leans down on the horn of his saddle, wipes his hand across his forehead and sighs. "That poor gal doesn't even know you ain't got a clue."

"She knows what I think about her."

"You tell her how you feel?"

"What sort of nonsense are you talking about?"

Griz sucks the whiskers under his lip into his mouth and chews. "Women like to know how you feel about 'em."

"I think you've been spending too much time with a certain type of recreational woman, on our dime."

"Whose dinero is it exactly?" Griz crinkles his brow.

Pack shrugs. "Well, Elliott is the one who found it."

"Don't matter. Women like it when you tell 'em."

"Tell 'em what?"

Griz rolls his eyes hopelessly and turns toward town. "You figure it out for yerself."

Trailing the extra saddle mount, Pack steers his horse after Griz. With a muddled look on his face, he complains. "Dammit, Griz! I wish you'd talk straight."

~*~

Mexico Sky

In the corner room of the hotel, Elliott still lingers in the bathing tub with a wash cloth covering over her face. Shimmering wet portions of her body emerge from the soapy depths of cloudy bathwater. The distinct clomping sound of a large group of horses approaching stirs her from her repose.

Removing the cloth from her face, Elliott sits upright in the tub. She stands to grab a folded towel from a nearby chair and wrap it around herself, before she steps out onto the second-story balcony. In the street below, the posse rides toward the building across the street from the hotel and stops.

Watching from above, Elliott holds her bath towel tight to her naked form and stares in disbelief, as the leader of the posse dismounts in a strange, but familiar way. "It can't be?"

The gentleman turns his steely gaze toward the saloon and hotel across the way. Elliott ducks down and slips back into her second floor room, watching from behind the curtain on the open door. Elliott gasps, "No… It just can't be."

Taking a step back from the patio door and windows, Elliott puts her backside to the wall and slowly slides her wet body down to a seated position on the rough wooden floor.

Hugging the towel tightly to her body, she shakes nervously. Finally, releasing her grip on the bath towel, she hides her face in her hands.

30

Climbing the stairs to the set of rooms above the saloon, Pack, holds a key in hand and looks at the brass number-ring. "Dang, Griz… Ya spared no expense, I see." He stops at the last door down the hallway and gives it a gentle knock. Hearing nothing, he gives another soft knock then puts the key into the lock, turns it and opens the door slowly. "Hello…? Elliott, are you decent?"

Peeking through the doorway, Pack notices the wash tub near the balcony doors and looks around the seemingly empty room. "Wonder where she went?"

The click of a hammer cocking catches his attention, and his eyes dart to the window. Fully dressed, but with her hair still wet, Elliott steps out from behind the long drapes and lowers her pistol. "Don't just stand there in the hallway... Git in here!"

Pack scans the empty hallway, before stepping into the privacy of the room and closing the door behind him. "Elliott? Is everything okay?" He watches her go to the bed and put her gun in the holster rig on top. As she buckles-on the gun-belt and turns to face him, Pack asks, "What's goin' on with you?"

"We have to get out of here."

"What's the rush?"

The metal entry lock scrapes, as Pack twists the key on the interior side of the hotel room door. As he glances over at Elliott, he moves across the room to examine the tub of bathwater by splashing the soapy film on top, with his hand. "Griz is getting a drink downstairs, and I was thinking of trying this bathtub to get that camel smell off me."

Keeping her hand over her holstered pistol, Elliott walks to the window to peek out. "They're here."   "Who's here?"

Thinking that he must be joking, she looks at him incredulously. "*Them.*"

"Oh... *Them?*"

He follows her over to the window and looks outside at the line of horses tied along the front of the building, opposite the hotel. "Jeez... There must be one hell of a reward offered up for the return of that money."

Elliott looks at him, concerned. "Yeah. Must be..."

"I wish we could get it. Maybe there's still some way..." He puckers his lips together, thinking and nodding his head in thought.

"Are you kidding me, Pack?"

"Maybe we could negotiate with them?"

She rolls her eyes. "Too late for that."

"Yeah, yer probably right... Too risky an option." Stepping back, away from the window curtain, Pack draws his pistol from his holster and checks to see that it is fully loaded. He draws another round from his cartridge belt and drops it in the empty chamber.

As Elliott watches him load six-around, she suggests, "Let's jest git Griz 'nd go." Hidden by the curtains, Elliott observes the posse cross the street and head toward the saloon. Turning to Pack, by the door, she whispers loudly, "Where are the horses at?"

"They're tied out front."

"You think of that plan all by yourself?"

He gives his gun a spinning twirl into his holster and gives her a stern look. "I figured on a bath before headin' out."

"Well, they're coming this way now."

Pack moves to the balcony and looks out. "Aww, shit! If they see Griz, they'll recognize him right off."

"Is there another way out of here?"

He smiles at her standing in the balcony doorway. "You're looking at it."

She shakes her head and looks over the edge of the second story balcony down to the horses in the street. "This happens to you more often than to most folks?"

"Only when I'm with you…"

~*~

Pack and Elliott creep along the balcony above the front stoop of the saloon, trying to keep their boots and spurs quiet on the decking. They look below to see several men from the posse hanging outside. Elliott stops and whispers to Pack. "What now? We can't jest climb down, right in front of them."

Pack looks back across the porch deck to the doors of their room. "What if you just slipped down and out through the barroom? I don't think they've ever seen you close-up…"

"I don't think that's a good idea."

"Why not?"

Elliott looks to the horses below, shaking her head. "Jest think of something else."

"We don't have a lot of options."

"I don't want to do it that way!"

Pack holds a hand to her mouth to shush her, when he hears a familiar voice down below. He peeks over the railing to see Fisk talking to one of the posse members. Speaking low, he takes Elliott by the hand and pulls her with him toward wall of the building. "Damn… Fisk is with 'em."

Relieved, Elliott smiles. Pack gapes at her odd reaction. "Why are you smiling?"

"It's good to know he's not dead."

"That doesn't help our situation any."

She looks out across the street to the town's row of wooden buildings and canvas-covered shacks. "Maybe they're not out to kill us, like we thought…?"

He gives her a sidelong glance, rolls his eyes, and peers over toward the front railing of the balcony, above the saloon. "It probably only means that he was just as eager to turn on us as Hank was." He quietly moves across the wooden deck to the low railing, peeks over, looks back and waves her closer.

She dips her chin in agreement and follows him. "Yeah… That's much more likely."

31

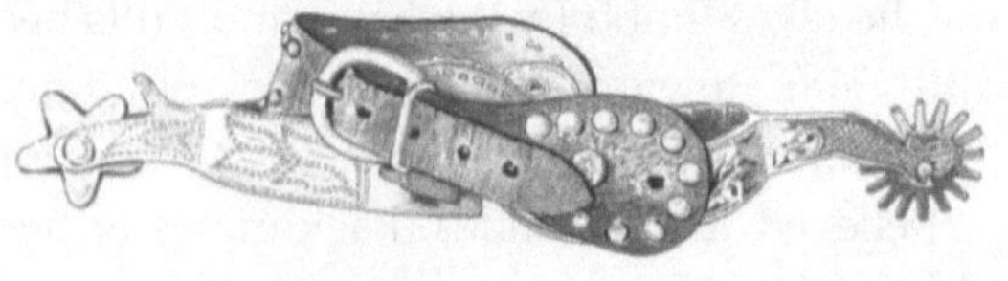

With his hat pulled down to conceal his features, Griz sits at a table at the back of the room, watching as the posse files into the saloon. He takes a sip from his shot of whiskey, while he eyes the horses hitched in front of the saloon. Taking a last big gulp, Griz wipes some dribble from his chin and pushes his chair back to stand. His gaze lowered to the floor, he starts the long walk to the front door.

Halfway across the room, Griz accidentally bumps into one of the posse members, and is brushed aside as the bounty-hunter continues on his way to join the others for a drink. Head tilted down, Griz makes his way outside and walks over to the line of saddle mounts secured in front of the building. He feigns drunkenness, as he leans down to untie Pack and Elliott's horses from the hitching rail.

Several posse members linger at the front entry of the saloon, and Griz steps around the horses to untether his own. Taking the reins in hand, he tosses them over his horse's neck. While putting a foot to the stirrup, he recognizes the voice of Fisk and inadvertently turns his head to look back as he swings up into the saddle.

Fisk, with a bandage around his middle and his arm in a sling, catches a quick glimpse of the old-timer and pauses in his conversation. He watches as the rider turns his horse away and takes a gander to the hotel balcony. "Hey you, old man... Hold it there a minute!" Fisk steps down into the street, to get a closer look, when the rider turns to him. "I'll be damned... We've been lookin' for you, Griz."

Shifting his hat on his head, Griz cracks a smile and looks up again to the saloon balcony. "Don't look now, Fisk." He watches, as Pack dangles Elliott out over the porch railing, just above the empty saddles of the two horses waiting below. Not heeding the warning, Fisk turns to look up just in time to see Pack swing Elliott toward him and let her go.

In a tucked ball of boots and britches, Elliott comes crashing down on top of Fisk, knocking him to the ground. Realizing Fisk is unconscious, she rolls off him and looks up to see the shocked expressions on the faces of the horsemen gathered near the entryway of the saloon. "Hello gentlemen... Jest had to drop in... Sorry I can't stay." She scrambles to her feet and leaps into the saddle of the nearest waiting horse, while Griz trots off down the street.

"C'mon girl! Let's git!"

Before the men can react, Elliott draws her pistol and fires several gunshots toward them. The boardwalk at their feet splinters, sending the men to find cover inside the saloon. She sees Pack throw a leg over the rail and stand on to the outer edge of the balcony. Elliott spins her horse in the street and hollers up to him. "Better jump for it!"

Pack considers the saddle horn and hard, leather seat directly below him and shakes his head. "Hell, no!"

She fires another pistol shot into the saloon, scattering the men away from the doorway, and smiles sweetly at him. "I'll still love you, no matter what..."

"Gol-dammit..."

"Go for it, Pack!"

He lets go of the porch rail, leans out over the saddled horse below and steps off the balcony. Pack drops down and wishbones onto the seat of the saddle with a heavy, gut-wrenching thud, causing the startled steed to bolt from the hitching post. Dust kicks up in the street, as the horse bucks to protest its sudden, unexpected burden.

Pack holds tight, looking sick as Elliott rides up beside him to settle his mount. "Wow, that was great! You alright?" His features are pale, as he leans over to vomit down her pant leg and over her boot. Elliott swats him with her pistol and curses. "Dammit, Pack! I just got the stink off me...!"

The members of the posse rush out onto the boardwalk and gawk at the horseback pair whirling in circles, right in the middle of the street. At the sound of gunshots, the well-dressed gentleman steps outside and is shocked to see everyone just standing around. "That's them we're after... Don't just stand there like idiots!"

Shaking the vomit off of her boot, Elliott gives Pack's horse a slap on the rump and gallops off after him and Griz. The men rush across the street to mount their tethered horses. Striding through the disorganized melee, the posse leader takes his horse by the bridle and leads it out of the crowd. Stokes rides up to join him, as the gentleman puts his foot to the stirrup, swings into his saddle and lifts a hand skyward. The swarm of horsemen assembles, as the leader sternly looks around. He swiftly motions forward after the departed riders, and the posse charges off, in pursuit.

32

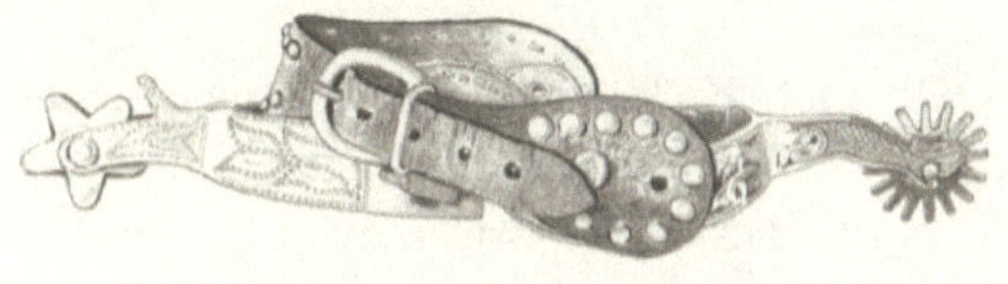

Steadily riding full-out, Pack and Elliott swiftly catch up with Griz to ride beside him, three abreast. As the old man bounces in his saddle, he looks over to notice Pack's pained expression. "You okay there, Pack?"

Spitting the vomit taste from his mouth, Pack keeps his seat tight to the saddle and grunts, "That flyin' mount took some out of me."

Elliott pats her leg and grumbles, "Yeah, I've got most of it here, still on my pants."

Griz looks down at Elliott's leg and winces in disgust. "Girl, if it ain't piss, its puke…"

She glares sourly at Griz and then over to Pack, who simply shrugs. Shaking her head in frustration, she looks past her shoulder to see the dust raised by the posse in pursuit. "Don't look now, but they're comin'!"

Riding hard, the three push on through the south Texas terrain, consisting of brush and scrub.

~*~

On foot, Pack, Elliott and Griz lead their horses through the moonlit landscape. Pack slows his pace to let Griz move up alongside him. "You gonna to be able to find this friend of yours in the dark?"

"Nope… But, if we keep on movin' toward the river, we might be there by mornin'."

Elliott joins them, looks into the starry night sky and asks Griz, "This guy have some sort of camp or home base that he works out of?"

"You could call it that. He calls it an airstrip."

Questioning, she looks at Griz. "What's that?"

Pack ponders the term, and then replies to her inquiry. "You mean for those aircraft machines?"

Griz nods to them and continues into the darkness. "Jest one, I think. He uses it to patrol the border region."

In wonderment, Elliott responds, "From the air?"

"That's what I think he's s'posed to be doin' at least. Mostly, he just fixes the thing and repairs bullet holes from folks shootin' at 'im from the ground."

Pack seems intrigued and eager to know more. "Hey, Griz… How'd you end up with a friend like that?"

"I got lots of odd friends. I even know a fella that has one of them fancy automobiles."

Flashing a bright smile in the darkness, Elliott retorts, "Aww, Griz… And here I thought we were the most interesting friends you had…."

His silver beard glisten in the moonlight, as the old man scratches it and winks at Elliott. "You're one of the few who gets shot at on a regular basis."

Hanging his head at the friendly jab, Pack mutters, "That's not how I planned on leaving town."

Elliott laughs. "It never is…"

~*~

The morning is bright and sunny, as three horseback fugitives approach the north bank of the Rio Bravo del Norte. The sloping shores are low and accessible from both sides of the shallow waterway. Pack waves his extended arm toward the river and comments, "O'er there is Mexico for you, Elliott! Which way we headed now, Griz?"

The old man studies the wild landscape and then turns to the rising sun. "I believe his setup is further down river."

They gape questioningly at the old-timer, and Pack comments, "Down river? We've almost run out of Texas..." He looks to Elliott and then over to Griz. "Is that jest a guess?"

"An educated one, mostly."

Elliott wipes a sleeve across her mouth to hide a smile. "I haven't heard you make one of those before."

Griz glances over at Elliott, winks broadly and smirks. "This old-fella still has a few tricks in 'im." He rubs his whiskers and then flaps his arms out, like he is going to fly. "Ol' Chadwick mentioned, once, that he could fly from his airstrip to the coast in a single day!"

Pack looks back over his shoulder to the north. "You sure he ain't base-camped closer to Laredo?"

"Don't think so, but I do like to spend time there when I can. If'n I had more of that bank money in my pocket, I could visit a lady-friend I had there a few dozen years ago."

Elliott smiles. "Let's find your other pal first."

Pack leans down on the horn of his saddle, pondering, and raises an inquisitive eyebrow toward Griz. "Did you say Chadwick was his name?"

"Yep. Chadwick Leightbottom, the aero-flyer."

Pack grins at the name. "You're kidding?"

"Nope! Couldn't make up a name like that."

Elliott shrugs and follows, as Griz leads the way southeast along the riverbank. "He better be light in the britches to get into one of them flyin' machines."

Pack looks back over his shoulder to scan both their back-trail and the horizon for any sign of the following posse. As he trots to catch up from behind, he calls ahead to Griz. "I'm jest curious… How long have you known this aircraft-flyin' fella, *Light-britches*?"

Continuing his course, Griz calls back over his shoulder, "*Leightbottom*… Not britches." Trotting along the riverbank, the old man peers behind at Pack. "Well, sonny-boy, I've known 'im longer'n you…"

33

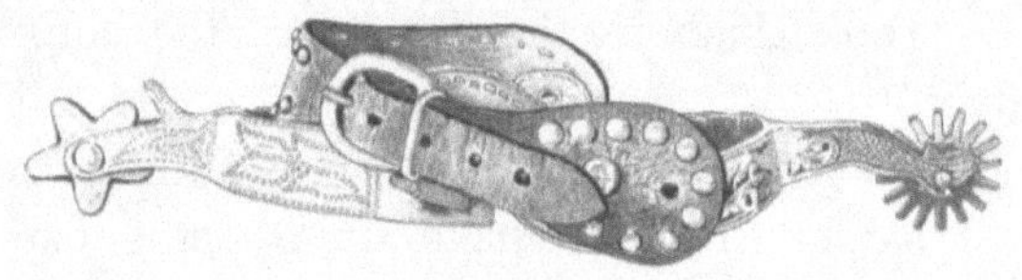

Weaving their way through thick underbrush and scrubby trees, Griz leads the way along the riverbank. Pack and Elliott duck, pushing away the scratchy limbs that block their path. Griz reins up his horse and stands in the stirrups to get a better view ahead. "Well, I'll be... That must be it."

As Elliott emerges from the thicket, she spots a small wood-framed shack near a shaded lean-to and a brush-cleared stretch of ground, bordered with piles of rocks. "That's a fancy setup for bein' way out here." As they sit their horses on the shoreline to gaze across a bend in the river, a low rumbling engine sounds, off in the near distance.

A double-stack, winged contraption flies toward them, cruising low over the winding river. The box-like kite slowly floats through the sky, aided by a power-plant and solitary propeller. Pack watches, and Elliott mutters with fascination, "Watchin' a man fly..."

Pack nods. "He must be nuts."

With a groan, Griz makes crazy-eyes at them, tugs at his whiskers and prods his horse onward. "That would be ol' Chadwick for ya..."

The aero-plane softly glides over the brush-cleared strip and the noisy engine cuts in short bursts before bumpily setting down on the rocky pathway.

~*~

As the airplane's engine sputters to a stop, the pilot removes his goggles and brown, leather skull-cap. Chadwick Leightbottom is a man in his middle years with a wild-eyed gaze and a tuft of messy hair to match. His lean frame almost seems to be an extension of the rickety aircraft he is piloting.

Stepping from his airplane, Chadwick watches as the three riders approach his basecamp from around the bend. With the sun behind, he narrows his gaze and tries to identify the visitors as they splash across a shallow bit of the river. Acting nonchalant, Chadwick tosses his goggles and headgear onto the seat of the plane and grabs a pistol from the cockpit. He puts it behind his back and waits.

~*~

They splash their horses through the shallows and trot up the embankment to the landing strip. At the forefront, as they crest the berm, Griz speaks aside to Pack and Elliott. "Now, Chadwick here don't get many friendly visitors about, so be watchful, with no quick movements…"

With a tranquil grin, Elliott eyes the aviator next to his flying machine. "Seems friendly enough…"

"You don't survive alone out here by bein' sociable."

Sticking close to the others, Pack nods his head and puts on a smile of his own. "Agreed."

Griz waves an arm, as they approach the airman and his plane. "Halloo there, Chadwick…!"

The pilot takes a moment to recognize the old-timer leading the visitors, and his shoulders visibly drop to a more relaxed position. Chadwick's vacant smile turns genuine, as he greets his old friend. "Well, hello to you, Griz... Kinda out of your territory, ain't ya?"

Griz beams and puffs out his chest. "Not by a long shot. I's got lady-friends both sides of the border needin' attention."

"Whatcha doin' here, and who are your pals?"

"Me and my pards here are headin' down to Mexico fer a visit, and was needin' some fresh water."

Suspicious, Chadwick puts a scrutinizing eye on them. "You may have noticed there's a river jest a few feet south?"

Griz shakes his bearded chin and hocks some spittle to the side. "No, not *that* wet-flow, runnin' with cattle shit and coyote piss... You told me one time 'bout a water-well that was run into the ground and tapped into an aquifer."

Skeptical, the pilot asks, "You lookin' for a bath?"

Insulted, Griz exclaims, "Hell no, I ain't!" He grumbles, "I was embarrassed enough askin' fer water fer these two tumbleweeds, when I *know* you must have a supply of home-brewed whiskey somewhere about."

Chadwick stares at the riders for a long, uncomfortable moment, before finally shifting his expression to his familiar smile. "Of course, Griz... Glad you stopped by for a visit." Pack and Elliott cautiously watch, as Chadwick brings the concealed pistol around from behind his back and tucks it in the leather belt around his waist. As Griz steps down, Chadwick gestures to the two companions, still horseback. "So, who are yer friends there?"

Griz gathers his reins and tilts his head toward Pack. "This here is Pack, an old runnin' pal from up in Montana." He slaps the end of his leather reins along the shaft of his tall boot and nods to the side. "And this is his trail-pard, Elliott."

The airman takes a step toward the lean-to and waves them along to follow. "Pleased to make your acquaintance. Step on down, and come out of the sun."

Elliott dismounts, whispering aside to her partners. "Sure is sociable enough, it seems..."

Pack swings a leg forward over the saddle horn and slides down. "Like a gila monster..."

Leading his horse to the watering barrel near the lean-to, Griz murmurs aside to them both. "He's jest full of color."

Elliott chuckles. "Sure does seem full of somethin'."

Pack nods in agreement. "Being out here all alone will do somethin' to ya, but I don't know if colorful is the word..." They follow Griz to the watering barrel, taking in the random assortment of government-labeled wooden crates scattered about the base camp.

34

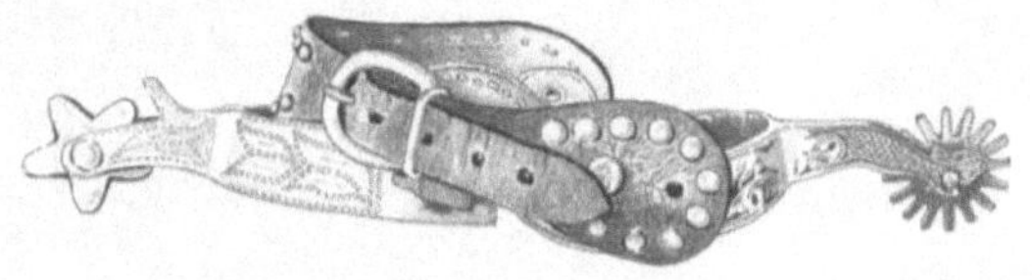

Under the shade of the lean-to, in a makeshift mechanic shop, boxes are filled with tools and custom-designed aircraft parts. The four of them relax, with full canteens of water, enjoying a breeze coming from across the slow-flowing river. Elliott takes off her cowboy hat and combs her fingers through her matted hair, while Pack glances around for any possible spots where the stolen money might be hidden.

Reaching over to one of the U.S. stamped crates, Chadwick flips the wooden top aside. He pulls out an unmarked bottle and shakes the liquid contents before tossing it to Griz. "I know you surely didn't come all this way for a sip of water. How about trying something a bit stronger?"

Examining the bottle, Griz rubs his hand across his mouth and licks his lips eagerly. "Now yer talkin'. Where's it from?"

"The locals across the river make it in trade."

Chadwick takes out glasses, and Griz returns the bottle. Pack turns his attention to them and asks, "Trade for what?"

The airman pauses a moment and looks to his guest. "Sir... That would be a matter of my own personal business." As he pours the first serving, his elusive answer gets Pack to thinking about this out-of-the-way border operation. Chadwick hands over a filled glass to Elliott in a most gallant way. "Excuse me, darlin', excuse my language, but it'll most likely put hair on yer chest if ya use it for more'n sippin'."

She takes the glass from the pilot and passes the drink under her nose for a sniff. "I've certainly had much worse." Taking a mouthful, Elliott gingerly swallows the beverage, rolls her shoulders up and back, then takes a deep breath. Pleased, Chadwick smiles at her and then pours one for Griz. "I like her... She's a keeper." He repeats the process again and hands a drink to Pack. Finally serving himself one as well, Chadwick settles into his leather-cushioned wicker chair. "Where're you all headed to?"

After taking a swig of his drink, Pack coughs a reply. "Jest down Mexico way… To spend some time on the coast."

Chadwick nods, takes a gulp and lets the warm beverage slide down his gullet, triggering a slight shiver. "Good time for it. The Mexes ain't been raiding or killing much this season."

His glass empty, Griz pokes his finger down inside and swipes it clean. "I warned 'em that it can get kinda rough."

Chadwick grins, and he offers up the bottle to Griz when he notices him lick his finger. "Yeah, it can get bloody down here sometimes." He refills Griz's empty tumbler and adds a bit more to his own. "When that happens, it's usually best to stick close to home."

Elliott takes another taste of her drink, winces as it burns her throat, and then sets it aside on a government crate. She looks at Chadwick, and her eyes connect with his briefly. Like a schoolgirl fascinated by a new teacher, she queries, "How is it that you can actually fly?"

Mexico Sky

The airman kicks up his long legs on a box, reclines in the chair and muses, "Actually, a lot of fellas have been developing machines to fly. You just never heard of them yet."

Taking a sipping drink, Pack tilts his head in disbelief. "I think we would've heard of it."

The airman raises an eye to Pack, as he fiddles with the tumbler balanced on his bent leg. "There are two brothers in the east that have a similar set-up. They're pretty good, but waste their time fixin' on bicycles and such."

Continuing her doe-eyed stare at the aviator, Elliott asks, "Why aren't you and your flying machine in a special exhibition somewhere like the World's Fair?"

Chadwick taps his boot toe on the side of a wooden box with the United States Government markings stamped on it. "This outfit didn't happen overnight. Special funds are allotted to support my habit and keep me testing manned-flight exclusively for them. In return, I live here, in the remotest part of the country, where only the jackrabbits can report on me."

She sighs. "Seems lonely…"

"Hardly. This kind of stuff can't be done with a committee breathing down your neck."

Looking at the airstrip and the camp in a different light, Pack nods his agreement. "Not too bad of an arrangement, being paid to do what you love and be left alone…"

The flyer shrugs nonchalantly and takes another drink. "It has its perks and its downsides."

Starting the feel a warm numbing sensation from the alcohol, Pack stands up to have a look around. "What's the downside?"

Chadwick changes his tone, ever-so-slightly, and stares at his guests. "Unexpected visitors, who might jeopardize my way of life…"

Elliott notices the change in the aviator's demeanor. "Like us…?"

He cuts away from his serious tone and takes a drink. "No, no… Any trusted friend of Griz is a sure friend of mine. My reference was to bandits and such." He nods to a new machine gun, on a tripod, poking out from under a tarp. "They mostly leave me alone now."

With a whistle, Pack takes a step over and lifts the corner of the tarp to examine the automatic gun more closely. "They ain't tried to steal this from you?"

"Sure they have… It's a real chore to load the thing, and I've already done away with some rascals that have tried to take it for their cause. I guess they didn't want it that bad, and I seem to have discouraged 'em."

Pack lowers the tarp and stares at the large bore of the barrel, still sticking out. "This thing up on one of your flying machines would sure be somethin'."

Chadwick grins, understanding the implication. "Yeah, that's what the military wants, too, but there's no good place to mount it and then operate the thing without throwing off the balance of the craft or shooting off my own propeller." He passes the bottle to Pack, who moves back to take a seat. The aviator smirks in his unnerving way and nods to them all. "Yer all welcome to spend the night, but I have to be flying again on the morrow. I have some business to attend to."

Griz cheerfully finishes off his generous second pour. "Sure do appreciate the hospitality."

As Griz raises his empty glass, Elliott interrupts his plea for more. "We have to be going. Sorry we can't stick around... Right, Griz?"

Pack and Elliott both look to their senior partner for confirmation, but he only licks his lips and looks fondly toward the remains in the bottle of Mexican home-brew. "Can't see why... Tomorrow is jest as well."

Studiously watching them all, Chadwick grins and raises his glass in a toast. "Tomorrow it is, then. Let's enjoy our brief bit of company for the moment."

35

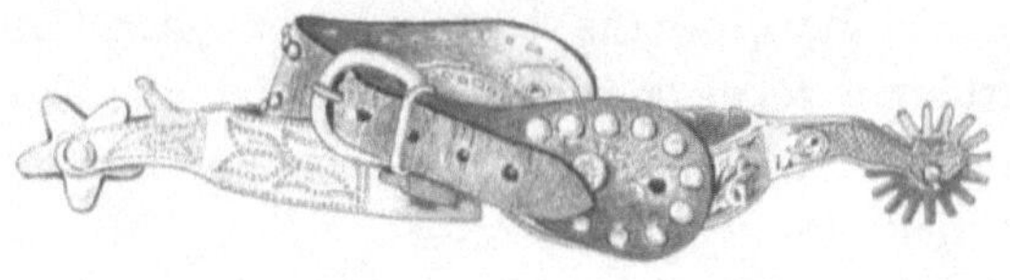

All is still in the aviator camp, as the purplish light of morning takes over the night sky. Near the lean-to tent, smoke trickles up from the ashes of the evening's fire. On foot, several men, with rifles at the ready, approach the airstrip. The leader of the posse leads several men forward, and the others slowly rise from the landscape to encircle the camp.

~*~

Inside the shack next to the lean-to, Pack and Elliott lay next to Griz, sleeping on bedrolls. The morning sunlight starts to stream through the cracks between wallboards and in through the door, revealing a stationary form in the entry. Elliott stirs from her hung-over slumber and looks to the bright doorway. She lets her eyes adjust to the glare of sunshine and recognizes the face of Chadwick staring at her. The daylight streams in, as he leans to the side and speaks. "Good mornin'... How's that pretty head of yours feeling?"

As she wipes the sleep from her eyes while trying to focus on his backlit features, she sees movement behind him. "It does hurt a mite. What's going on?"

Chadwick glances back to his basecamp and shrugs. "Well, it looks like y'all overstayed your visit."

The leader of the posse steps into the sunlit doorway, next to the aviator, and stares down at her. "Hello Elliott... Funny meeting up with you like this. After all this time apart, I expected better for you."

She stares at back at him, not appearing too surprised. "Yeah... I guess our expectations aren't what they used to be. Thought you were still dead?"

The mysterious gentleman steps aside from the door and several men from the posse enter with their rifles cocked. Elliott snorts and kicks her foot out to wake her partners. "Hey, Pack 'nd Griz, we have some company here in camp." As they slowly wake from sleep, the first thing they see is the butt of a rifle slamming them into unconsciousness.

~*~

Outside on the ground, with their hands tied behind them, the three prisoners lean back on wooden supply crates. A posse member reclines in Chadwick's wicker chair, guarding them with a rifle across his lap. Under the warm midday sun, the man's eyelids grow heavy, and he nods-off frequently during his watch.

With his temples throbbing in pain as he slowly rouses to consciousness, Pack blinks his eyes open to focus. He looks around to see men seated around the campfire and Chadwick standing to the side, talking to the gentleman. Elliott looks over to Pack, as Griz starts to come around. "Sorry, Pack..."

"For which part?"

She shrugs, with a feeble smile. "All of it..."

Pack nods sluggishly, wincing from the excruciating pain in his head, while he assesses their unfortunate situation. "Did I hear correctly that their leader knows you?"

"Yes."

"Should I even ask where from?"

Looking sheepish, Elliott digs her boot heels into the hard, sandy ground. "He's my husband."

Pack looks to Elliott to confirm that she isn't joking. "Your husband?"

"Yes..."

"I thought you said he was dead?"

"Yeah... I thought he was."

Pack turns to look at the gentleman talking to the aviator and whispers quietly to Elliott. "How did he end up at the head of this posse?"

Disheartened, Elliott's shoulders slouch as she replies, "I don't know... About twelve years ago, I was informed that he was deceased, and I never had any reason to question it."

"Until now?"

"Yeah... Until now."

Pack closes his eyes to ease the piercing pain in his temples and then turns to look at her inquisitively. "What do you think he's gonna to do with us now?"

"How should I know?"

"He's your husband."

She glares at Pack, unamused, and then turns as Chadwick finishes his conversation with the leader of the posse and strolls over to them. "Guess we're about to find out. Here comes Chadwick."

"Don't trust that sneaky bastard."

Elliott nods and snorts. "I wouldn't start now."

Chadwick hooks his thumb at the guard, and ushers him to leave. After checking for approval from his boss, the guard gets up and moves away. The flyer pulls up his chair to sit by the prisoners. Dusting off the top of his boots with a sweep of his hand, he looks them over. "Griz, you alert yet?" Raising his head slightly, Griz sighs and grunts affirmative. Sitting closer, Chadwick sees that a trickle of blood on the old man's temple has run down and dried to a crust in his beard. "That hit on the head hurts worse than the hangover, I bet..."

The old-timer tilts his head and moans, "I've had enough of both to even 'em out."

The aviator chuckles at his friend's sporting reply and turns to Pack and Elliott. "What are we to do here?"

Pack narrows his eyes at Chadwick and responds, "Suppose you work for that fella now, eh?"

"No, but I am in the business of my own survival. Being on this side of things suits me a whole lot better than where y'all are sitting."

Elliott tosses her hair back. "What do you want?"

"What I want is for all of you to be out of here." Chadwick leans in closer. "The thing *they* want is a certain amount of stolen money from a holdup. Seems they had plans on doing the job themselves and someone beat them to it."

Elliott clenches her jaw and stares up at the aviator. "We didn't rob that bank."

"Doesn't matter… They think you have the money, so you need to come up with something."

Pack shakes his head. "We don't have it."

"I know." Chadwick turns from Pack and Elliott, and looks to where Griz sits with his head hanging down slightly. "This sounding at all familiar, Griz? Do you really think you could stash something like that in my supply wagon, and I wouldn't happen upon it at some point?"

Griz stares down at his boot tops, as he grumbles to his old friend. "Thought it would be safer with you than me…"

"Oh, it's safe alright."

Elliott turns to Griz and then looks back to Chadwick. "Where is the money hidden now?"

"That's the problem…"

She is confused. "What's the problem?"

"It's gone."

The prisoners stare blankly at Chadwick, until Pack finally utters, "What do you mean, *gone*?"

Chadwick shrugs casually. "I spent it."

Elliott blurts out, "On what?!?"

"Doesn't really matter now, does it? Why is it that womenfolk always seem interested in the wrong details?" Shaking his head and lounging back in the creaking chair, Chadwick rubs the whisker stubble of his unshaven chin. "What you should be asking is, what are they gonna do with you when they find out you don't have any of that money?"

They all glance to the leader of the posse standing near the others at the campfire, and Elliott asks, "What *are* they going to do?"

Kicking out his feet, Chadwick crosses his arms and shrugs. "I don't really know… I told him I would try my best to find out where y'all hid it. I'll just tell him I did my best, and you'll be on your own." Chadwick studies Elliott astutely. "He seems especially interested in you for some reason."

Starting to come around and a bit more clear-headed, Griz looks up and growls, "Leave her alone."

Chadwick frowns at Griz, but nods in agreement. "Would love to take y'all along with me, but I have to go. And, you seem tied-up with other business."

Behind his back, Pack strains at the ropes wrapped around his wrists. "Where are you going off to?" The aviator stands, brushes the leg of his pants and smiles. "I gotta fly." He gives a wave and struts over to give a report to the boss.

The two men chat momentarily and Chadwick shakes his head, unhappily. The captives watch, as the aviator puts on a show of virtuousness, then shrugs innocently and walks away to his parked flying machine. He glances back to the captured guests and offers a smiling wink. Pack looks at Griz and then over to Elliott. "Between Griz's old acquaintances and your former husbands, things couldn't turn out much worse, now could they?"

Elliott looks surprised. "Husbands? Just one!"

"That's enough!"

Griz silently chews on his lip whiskers, and Elliott, trying to remain upbeat, responds. "We could always resort to plan B."

Confused, Pack looks at her. "What's that?"

"Shoot our way out."

Considering how they are all sitting in a row, with their hands tied behind their backs, he asks. "And how would that happen exactly?"

"I surely don't know, Pack... But, you'll think of something."

36

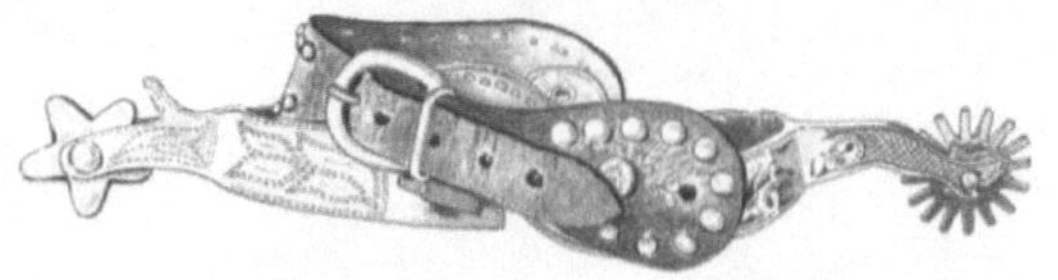

The cooling shadow of the lean-to moves slowly past the three captives, as the day wears on. Pack, Elliott and Griz watch helplessly, as Chadwick packs up his aeroplane and prepares to fly out. Elliott shakes her head at him, murmuring, "That son of a bitch..."

Pack glances at her. "I really can't blame him much." As the words leave his mouth, he looks accusingly at Griz.

Downcast, the old-timer replies, "Sorry, you two... Thought we would git down here 'nd grab that stashed money before he even noticed."

A soft shuffle of feet, from behind, puts them on alert, and Pack tenses at the touch of a hand on his shoulder. Squatting directly behind them, hidden by the supply crates, Hank flicks open the blade of a folding knife. Keeping low and out of sight, he whispers, "Shh, don't speak or look back." One at a time, he slips the sharp edge between the ropes that bind their wrists, cutting them free.

Griz raises an eyebrow at Pack, and Elliott breathes a sigh of relief. Over her shoulder, she whispers, "What are you doing here, Hank?"

"Jest following the money, that's all."

They look at him surprised and she utters, "Still?"

"You know me, darlin'. Always..." Pack and Elliott rub their sore wrists behind their backs, while studying the positions of the men about the camp. Hank folds his knife and crouches low behind Elliott. "Where is it stashed?"

She faces ahead and replies. "We still ain't got it."

Disappointed, Hank drops his chin to his chests. "You're kidding... *Really*? I thought you gave it to Griz?"

Griz grunts, "Money is really hard to come by these days..."

Hank hisses softly, "Who has it now?"

Pack nods his head forward toward the aviator prepping his flying machine. "The fella with the aero-plane has it."

"Hell, you guys are the worst."

Pack glances behind to Hank, and whispers snidely, "We *tried* to turn it in."

"You sure didn't do that very well either."

They all look forward, as the leader of the posse checks his timepiece, looks up and walks toward them. On his way, he kicks at the sleeping man on guard duty. Hank eases further back amongst the supply crates, as the gentleman stops, to address them. "So, our flying friend tells me you won't reveal to him the location of the money."

Pack stares back, considering him in the new light of being Elliott's long-assumed dead husband. "What's to tell? We don't have it."

The gentleman turns his stare away from Pack and over to Elliott. "I have often thought about how I should have taken you with me when I left. Who knew you would have sunk so low?"

Elliott looks up with a sneer. "Look who's talking. What are you, a corrupt lawman now?"

"Not a lawman... I work for special interests."

"What interests are those?"

"My own."

"You haven't changed at all."

"Most men don't want to. Women always assume they can change a man somehow."

Pack interrupts the marital squabble with a question of his own. "What about all these guys? You going to split the robbery money with all of them?"

"These men are all hired guns and, thus, disposable. They are simply riding along for the promised cash reward." The gentleman glances over his shoulder, lowering his voice so as not to be overheard, and states, "Good men, all of them. Don't get me wrong... but, merely employees with no thoughts of the bigger picture."

Sensing a con artist greater than himself, Pack is intrigued by the gentleman. "What's the big picture?"

"The heist from the bank was planned for months, before that ill-fated robbery occurred, and you went and bungled it further. But, no matter... I still want my money."

Elliott looks up at her former husband and implores, "We had nothing to do with it, and *we don't have the money!*"

The gentleman's probing gaze passes over the group and finally rests on Griz, who scowls and then turns away. "But *he* knows where it is." He takes out a pocket revolver, cocks it and aims at Griz. "Where can I find the money?"

Pack looks at Griz and then back up to the man. "Intimidation won't help us know something we don't."

The tiny pistol fires and hot lead tears into Griz's thigh. He jumps in pain, clenching his untied hands behind his back. Elliott cries out, "Stop it!! We'll find the money for you."

Her ex-husband looks at her dolefully, shaking his head. "We've followed you all to Mexico, and I want it now. Tell me where it is, or I start putting bullets into these two."

As he turns the direction of his second shot to Pack, Elliott blurts out, "It's on the aero-plane."

He looks over his shoulder to where Chadwick is preparing to leave, and looks back at her. "Huh… Really?"

"Yes…"

The man standing over them shakes his head and sighs. "Unfortunately, we already searched the camp and aircraft. Nice try, Elliott." He keeps the small revolver pointed at Pack.

She quietly utters, "We don't have it…"

Noticing that Elliott is about to cry, the leader of the posse lowers the barrel of his gun and sneers at her. "Elliott, you have feelings for this saddle-bum?" He raises the pistol up again. "Too bad…"

She calls out, "Don't! Please…!"

The hint of a smile teases on the gentleman's lips, and he cocks back the hammer of his handgun before replying, "Now that I have what I want, why would I not kill him?"

37

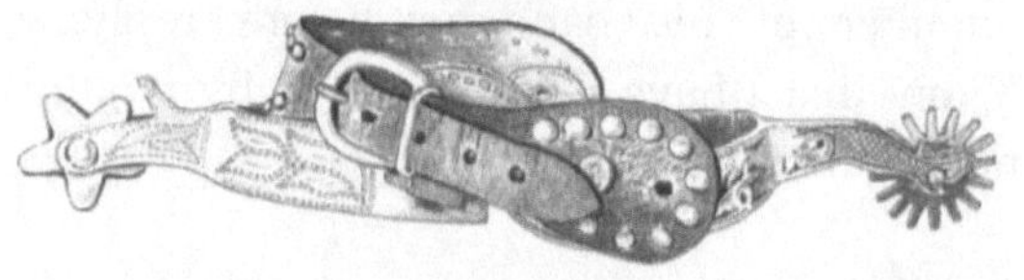

Stepping into the broken shade of the lean-to, Fisk levers a round into his rifle and raises it up to his shoulder. Everyone turns their attention to the wounded man, as he directs his aim at the posse leader. "Hold it right there, you bastard."

The tip of the rifle-barrel motions toward the ground, and Fisk sternly instructs, "Put that gun down, or I'll shoot." The captives lined upon the ground watch attentively, as the leader of the posse uncocks the hammer and lowers the pistol. Fisk shakes his head and exclaims. "Not you, dummy… *Him!*"

The gentleman looks back to the hostages. "Who?" Rising from his hiding spot behind the wooden supply crates, Hank stands and slowly raises both hands up to chest level. Incredulous, the gentleman gasps out. "Is that the man from the watering hole?"

In a blur of motion, Pack lunges forward, tackles Elliott's former husband to the ground and tries to wrestle the small handgun away from him.

Fisk lowers the aim of his rifle to direct it at Pack. Quickly moving around the crates, Hank grabs hold of the end of Fisk's barrel and pulls it away. He slams his other fist into his partner's neck and the blasting rifle shot goes astray, alerting everyone in camp to the scuffle.

As Pack rolls with Elliott's husband on the ground, she scoots over to attend to Griz and his leg wound. The old-timer, clutching a rag at his bloody thigh, pushes her away. "Don't worry 'bout me... Get somethin' to defend yerself!"

Elliott realizes that the posse members are all grabbing for their weapons. She ducks away when a gunshot splinters the corner of a crate near her arm, and as she scoots back she bumps into the large caliber machine gun. As the posse begins to take up shooting positions, around them, she quickly considers the mounted gun.

Dramatically tearing off the tarp covering, she takes a firm stance behind the automatic gun and pulls back the bolt. Armed men advance on the lean-to and Elliott pulls the heavy trigger on the gun to a disappointing *click*. Several men laugh, as they shoulder their rifles and continue to move toward her.

Suddenly, she is forcefully pushed aside and a familiar voice whispers from over her shoulder. "Here, ma'am... Allow me." Chadwick leans over the gun, feeds a belt of ammunition into the magazine and claps the breech shut. Jerking back the bolt, he slams in a load, and bows gallantly, as he takes a step back. "There ya go. All set!"

She looks at him with wide-eyed amazement, and moves behind the automatic gun to take hold of the trigger. With a firm squeeze, several rounds pop off and whiz harmlessly into the nearby brush.

Several posse members cluster around Pack, as he fights with Elliott's spouse. One of the men swings a rifle butt into the fray and catches Pack in the ribs, knocking the wind out of him. The posse leader quickly climbs to his feet and delivers a heavy kick to Pack's torso. Elliott pivots the gun barrel and bellows, "Back off! All of y'all!"

Several of the hired gunmen shake their heads with uncertainty at the female standing behind the machine gun. "Damn, she's jest a woman..."

Wise enough to recognize the power of a woman's wrath, Chadwick steps back a few more paces and declares. "Fellas, I would advise you not upset her."

Assisting his boss, Stokes glares at Elliott, as he waves several of his men toward her. "Somebody get her off that gun, before she hurts someone!" He grabs the gentleman's hat up from the ground, dusts it off and hands it back to him. Elliott's husband turns to glower at her, as she stands firmly behind the automatic weapon.

Pack, still recovering from the kick to the chest, slowly gets himself up from the ground and turns to look at Elliott. They exchange a meaningful glance, just as one of the posse members moves past him and slaps the butt of his rifle across Pack's shoulders. Noticing a distinct change in Elliott's demeanor, Chadwick quickly dives to the side.

At the same instant, Pack and the husband both recognize the fury in Elliott's eyes. The posse leader dashes for cover and Pack flattens himself to the ground, as Elliott grits her teeth and squeezes the trigger. There is a deafening explosion of automatic machine-gun fire, and several of the gunmen tumble to the ground.

Elliott sprays the basecamp with gunfire and every able-bodied man dives for cover. Hank and Fisk, still tussling, break apart from another and are awestruck by what they see. Fisk swipes a smear of blood from his nostril and stutters, "Holy shit, Hank! She must be out of her damned mind?" Taking advantage of the distraction, Hank delivers a knock-down blow that sends his partner reeling to the ground.

Tentatively taking her finger from the trigger, Elliott and Hank exchange a promising look. He smirks, as he notices Pack on the ground crawling toward them, then utters. "That is one lucky damn fella…"

In the corner of his eye, Hank sees Fisk grab his dropped rifle from the ground, lever it and take aim at Elliott. Fisk narrows an eye and pulls the trigger. Without thinking, Hank dives at Elliott in attempt to push her away but his body blocks the path of the bullet. Hank tumbles to the ground, grasping at the wound to his stomach. In dismay, Fisk looks down at Hank and cries. "Damn, pard! Why'd you do that?" Levering his rifle again, he turns away from Hank on the ground, and positions himself to take another shot at Elliott.

From the cover of the supply crates, Chadwick sees Hank clutching his bullet-torn abdomen as Pack crawls closer. When he sees Fisk raise his rifle toward Elliott again, he kicks his foot out to the hot-smoking barrel of the machine gun. Unexpectedly pivoting with the automatic weapon as it swings around, Elliott holds on tightly and her finger squeezes on the trigger. As the gun spins, a spray of large caliber projectiles arc in a sweeping pattern across the airfield. Fisk catches several bullets across his chest, and the rifle falls from his grasp as he tumbles back.

His abdomen bleeding profusely, Hank crawls over to Fisk and rolls him over. The two friends gaze at each other complacently, and Hank frowns. "I'm sorry 'bout this, pard." Fisk nods agreeably and takes his last dying breath. "Yeah... Be seein' ya, Hank." Fisk's eyes glaze over, and his lifeless body falls limp, while his spirit drifts away to the sound of random gunshots and bullets whizzing overhead.

38

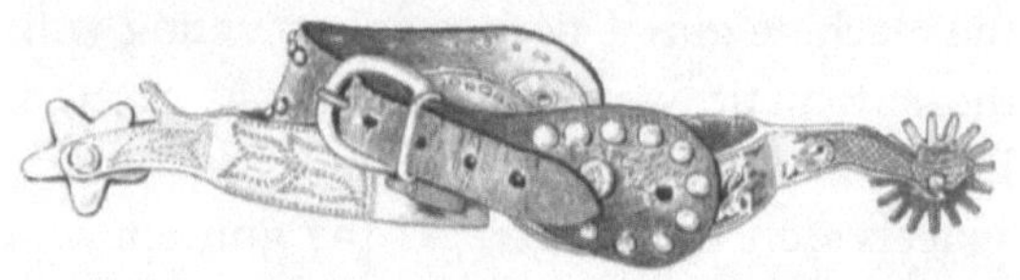

Between bursts of machine gun fire, Pack climbs to his feet. As he moves closer to Elliott and the machine gun, he sees the posse leader come out from hiding with a pistol aimed at him. Pack lifts his empty hands skyward and the well-dressed gentleman calls out to him, "You don't deserve her!"

Pack steadies for the impending gunshot and replies, "At least I stick with her."

"Doesn't really matter now…"

The gentleman clicks back the hammer of the pistol and takes careful aim. Just as he is about to fire, Elliott swings the machine gun around toward him. Without hesitation, she pulls the trigger only to hear the empty click of the receiver. "Nooo!"

The truant husband looks over at Elliott and smiles a broad, entertained grin. "It just wasn't meant to be, darling." In anguish, Elliott stares at him from behind the machine gun. He narrows an eye and is about to shoot, when a bullet tears into his side, under his arm.

Stumbling back, the leader of the posse turns to see Griz levering another round into the chamber of a rifle. The old-timer grins from under his bushy beard and waves. "There you go Packey, best we be gettin' out of here now." Shots continue to whiz all around them, as the posse regroups.

The wounded leader aims at Griz and hammers-off his last shot. The old-timer takes the bullet directly in the upper chest and slumps to the ground, dead.

Before the posse leader can reload his gun, Pack rushes forward and tackles him to the ground. Elliott stands in shock, as the men two fight it out, near to where Griz is splayed out, under the lean-to. Chadwick rushes over with another belt of ammunition for the machine gun and promptly swings the loaded receiver back in her direction. "Honey, be sure not to put any extra holes in that aero-plane of ours. It's our way out of here." He slaps her across the shoulders and dashes to untether the aircraft from its ground ties.

Pack continues to fight with Elliott's husband, smashing his fist repeatedly into the gunshot wound under his arm. After delivering a driving punch, Pack releases his grip, and the posse leader's head bounces back on the hard-packed ground, knocking him out cold. Pack, straddled atop him with nothing left to fight, looks over toward Elliott as she lets off several more bursts of machine-gun fire.

Staying low, Pack grabs a pistol from the ground, checks the load and rushes to Elliott's side. She looks at him with relief and utters, "Are you okay, Pack?"

He opens the gun to reload the pistol and grumbles, "I'm gettin' a little tired of shootin' our way out of things..."

Elliott grins fondly, as she clicks the trigger, pushing the members of the posse back with another smattering of gunfire. "With you, Pack, I wouldn't have it any other way."

The sound of an engine starting catches their attention, and Pack looks up to see Chadwick climbing into his aircraft. "Where the heck is he going?"

He raises his pistol aim toward the aero-plane and, between burst of gunfire, Elliott calls out, "Don't shoot him! He may be our best way out of here."

"In that thing?"

Elliott releases another blasting of gunfire and hollers, "Do you want to die here?"

He lowers his aim and looks at her as if she is crazy. "Do you want to die in that thing?"

Lovingly, she beams at him, winks and gazes skyward. "At least we'll be close to heaven..."

Pack tilts his head in reply. "You really think that's where we're headed?"

"What? Are you afraid of heights?"

"I'm not worried about the going up... It's the comin' down that hurts." He scoots closer to her at the machine gun and nudges her aside. "Go ahead and go. I'll cover you."

"No, we can both go!"

"Not a chance. I'll stay with Griz."

Elliott looks to Griz, who, despite the tragic bullet wounds, looks like he is peacefully sleeping. With both hands, she takes hold of Pack's face and turns him to stare directly into his eyes. "I need you to come with me." Elliott leans in and lays a passionate kiss on his open lips.

Pack lets her surprisingly romantic gesture linger a short while, before shaking it off. He squeezes a burst from the machine gun toward one of the posse members firing at them from behind some of the crates. Noticing her teary eyes when he looks back at Elliott, he nods his consent. "Okay, I'll go… But, I still don't like the idea of me flying."

Through the tear-streaked grime on her cheeks, she beams cheerfully and hugs Pack tightly around the neck. "Pack… I love you!"

"Yeah… Now scoot yer bottom over to that flyin' rig, and I'll cover for you."

"You're comin', right?"

Pack takes aim at a posse member and releases another burst of gunfire. "Get that damned thing going, and I'll be there as soon as I can."

Gunshots splinter chips of wood from the stack of crates behind them. Pack pulls Elliott off from around his neck and urges her toward the landing strip. He clicks off a few more rounds from the gun, when she stops, comes back, and gives him another loving kiss on the cheek. Pack wipes his face, pushes her away, and fires another burst from the gun. "Get going already!"

39

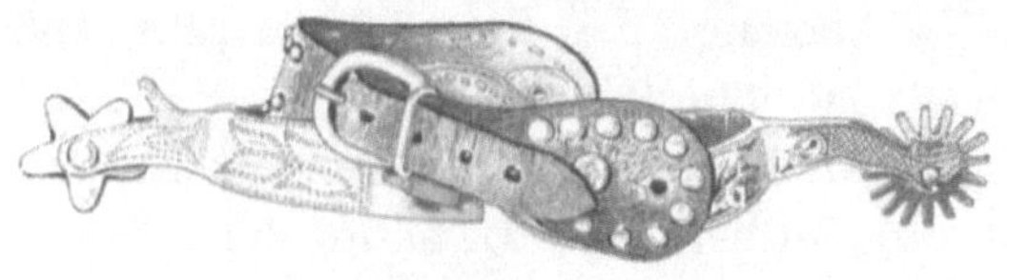

The aircraft engine is fired-up and Chadwick feathers the throttle forward, bringing the engine growl to a solid roar. Free from the tie-down lines, the plane starts to roll forward and the aviator steers it toward the runway. Dust swirls back with the prop-wash, as Elliott runs alongside looking for a place to climb in. She calls out over the noise of the engine, "We're coming with you!"

Chadwick lowers his goggles from his forehead to his eyes to fend off the blowing dust. He points a finger to the lower wing, where it connects along the airplane's body. "Grab on, and hold tight." He leans out of the single-seat cockpit and waves his hand toward a spot just above the wheel strut. "Get close to me as possible, to keep our balance."

The engine revs while the aircraft pivots and Chadwick positions the aircraft to face the path of runway. As the propeller blade whirls in front of them, Elliott lies on the cloth-covered wing and grabs hold of the leading edge. Looking up at the pilot she yells, "We need to wait for Pack!"

Chadwick shakes his head and pushes the throttle further forward, steering the aircraft off the rutted taxiway. "There's no time... We have to go!" Reaching the smooth, packed surface of the airstrip, the airplane lunges forward. Elliott turns to see Pack still using the machine gun to hold the posse members at bay, while bullets fly all around them. Holding on tightly, while the dusty draft from the spinning propeller pushes tears across her face, she calls out to him. "*PACK...!*"

~*~

Pack fires the machine gun from the lean-to and sees sand gust from the plane moving forward. He grits his teeth, when he sees the aircraft stop to linger briefly at the edge of the runway. "Dammit girl... Go, already!" Propeller whirling, the engine roars and lurches the airplane onward to the brush-cleared airstrip.

His next burst of gunfire goes astray, as Pack is violently pushed aside from behind the weapon. As he tumbles to the ground, Pack glances up to see Hank move into position behind the machine gun. His torso stained with blood, Hank is worse for wear, as he takes aim at a small cluster of riflemen firing back at them.

When an extended blast from the auto gun scatters every posse member for cover, Hank looks down at Pack. "This is the second time in a week I've had to cover yer ass. Let's not let it happen again." Pack turns from his old associate to the airplane beginning to taxi down the runway. Hank follows his look and waves Pack onward after them. "You better go after that girl before she finds someone better."

Pack draws his gun, shoots and yells. "I'll stay here and finish this!"

"What the hell is wrong with you?"

"I won't make it."

"Don't be a wuss! Sure you can!" Hank lets off a burst of gunfire that skitters across the surface of the ground, sending rocks and dirt flying up into the air. "Don't you spend all that money, 'cause I'm still comin' for my share!" The two men exchange a brief look of mutual respect, before Pack climbs to his feet and looks to the departing airplane. Hank shakes off the hurt from the bullet wound in his gut, and hammers another burst of gunfire at the remaining posse. "Go on and git, you dumb bastard..."

Taking a deep breath, Pack prepares himself to make the precarious dash for the runway. "Good luck to ya, pard." Gun in hand, he lunges from cover and sprints across the open area toward the moving airplane. Bullets whiz past him, as he high-steps it through the camp.

~*~

The aircraft starts to gain speed as it roars along the airstrip. The propeller blasts back a dusty cloud and Elliott looks behind to see Pack running full-out. Suddenly, three horsemen come bursting from the sagebrush in hot pursuit. Elliott yells to Chadwick, "Slow down, Pack's comin'!"

Without looking back, the aviator continues to work the levers and pedals to keep the aircraft on a straight course. He pushes the throttle forward and shouts, "Hell, no!" Through the noise from the aircraft engine, he hears the click of a firearm and looks over to see Elliott, with a pistol propped on the side of the fuselage, aiming at his face. Glancing past his shoulder, Chadwick sees Pack running with the three horsemen gaining on him. "Are you kidding me?"

"No, I'm not… Slow it down!"

With his hand still grasping the throttle, Chadwick briefly considers the consequences, and then pulls back the lever to slow up the airplane. Seconds pass painfully, as Pack redoubles his effort, and finally makes it to the aircraft wing. As he grabs the lower fuselage, Chadwick simultaneously shoves the throttle forward. The aircraft engine chugs, rumbles and roars with power, nearly jerking Pack loose from his grasp on the wing support strut.

Chadwick smiles to himself, as Pack clings on alongside and Elliott lowers her pistol. One of the horsemen rides up beside the speeding airplane, levers his rifle and shoots a round through the body of the aircraft. As he cocks his rifle again, Elliott swings her arm out and fires a series of gunshots, and the wounded the rider drops from his mount. The unmanned horse continues to run alongside for a few galloping strides, while the posse member tumbles and is lost in their dusty wake.

The increasing speed of the airplane slowly distances them from the other two pursing riders. The aircraft lifts from the ground, lightly skipping and bouncing off the runway at the mercy of the rising current of wind. Pack turns forward, grips tightly, and closes his eyes.

Elliott holds onto the wing strut, as the airplane gradually climbs higher. Looking down she can see Hank in the lean-to, beside the wood shack, still holding off the posse. The airplane banks away and she raises her hand to wave a heartfelt goodbye. As the plane departs, Hank lifts a bloody hand skyward in a final farewell salute.

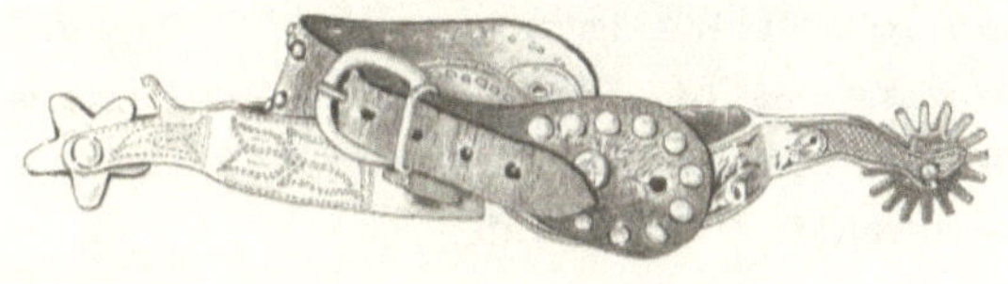

40

In flight, just over the treetops and sagebrush, the makeshift aircraft powers steadily along. Like a strange bird in the sky, the airplane soars eastward along the river valley toward the gulf coast. The flying machine lifts and drops as it rides the wind currents, tilting its wings over the isolated landscape while the engine steady drones on.

Embracing the newfound thrill of flying, Elliott looks down as the countryside beneath them races by. With tear-streaked eyes, she takes in the view before turning to peek over the fuselage in search of Pack. From the cockpit, Chadwick looks at her with a questioning eye as the wind whips against him. Elliott tries to look past the pilot, to the opposite wing, and hollers, "Is Pack still over there?"

Chadwick tilts his head to Pack's side of the airplane, then looks over to Elliott and flashes a sly grin with a nod. Sighing with relief, she smiles at the man behind the controls of the flying machine. The wind rushing past her, Elliott looks across the river toward Mexico, holds tightly to the wing, and settles in to enjoy the ride.

~*~

A lone, single-mast sailboat sits moored in an inlet, linked to the warm ocean waters of the Gulf of Mexico. Twenty yards from an isolated stretch of white-sand beach, the unattended sailing vessel looks peacefully picturesque. The grumbling roar of an engine is heard in the distance and the outline of the primitive airplane appears on the horizon. Several birds take flight from their roosting on the shoreline, as the aircraft flies low over the open stretch of beach.

Inside the aircraft, the aviator works the rudder controls and steers the flying machine over the calm waters before banking the wings for a gliding return to land. Moisture glistens in Elliott's eyes, as she takes in the sight of the blue waters and white sandy beaches below. The airplane engine cuts in and out, sputtering, while Chadwick works the throttle back and forth to slow their flight.

Approaching from low over the water, they drop down for a landing on the beach. The narrow wheels cut into the wet, hard-packed sand and the airplane touches down twice before settling in for a soft landing. Elliott shields her eyes from the wind and sea spray, streaming from the propeller, as the airplane's wheels sink hub deep into the sand.

Finally settled on the shore, the sensation of soaring lingers while the engine sputters, chugs and quits. Their ears slowly adjust to sounds other than the drone of the airplane and the hot, hissing tick of the engine. Elliott looks at Chadwick while she regains her senses, and suddenly feels the airplane settle further down in the soft sand of the beach. "Uhh... We seem to be sinking..."

"Yep... Won't be able to take off again."

"What?"

"With all of us aboard, we're way too heavy."

"Why did you land us here then?"

"This is it... Last stop."

Stepping around from the other side of the airplane, Pack appears woozy and unsure on his feet, tripping in the sand. Feeling nauseous, he braces himself on the tail-section. Elliott slides down from the wing and faces Chadwick. "You're not going to leave us here on the beach, are you?"

A pistol barrel pokes out from the cockpit, and the pilot eases his arm over the side of the airplane, aiming the gun. "That's exactly what I'm going to do." He points the firearm at Pack and motions for him to move over next to Elliott.

Raising his hands in surrender, Pack stumbles through the sand, uttering. "Huh... I sure didn't see that coming." Elliott looks disparagingly at Pack and turns to Chadwick. The flyer stifles a cough, and then takes a long, deep breath. He winces and, with the tip of the gun, motions them closer. "Help me out of here."

They are alarmed to see the aviator lay his head back, close to passing-out. Stepping forward to the airplane, Pack sees a pooling of blood in the pilot's lap. He dips his arm into the cockpit and wraps it around behind Chadwick.

From behind, Elliott tries to help Pack lift the airman from the flying machine. She gasps when she sees the smear of blood staining the seat. "Oh my, you're shot?" A beam of sunlight pokes through the fuselage where the rifle bullet had passed through. Chadwick rallies briefly and smiles at Elliott. "How nice of you to notice, darling."

Supporting the pilot from both sides, Pack and Elliott move him from the plane. They are about to set him down, when he shakes his head and points farther down the beach. "Not here... Over there."

Stumbling through the sand with the limp airman in tow, Pack and Elliott make their way toward the mouth of the inlet, nearer to where the sailboat is moored. As they pause to catch their breath, Elliott looks to her partner with concern. Momentarily alert, Chadwick opens his eyes and looks around. "Why are we stopping?"

Winded, Elliott responds while catching her breath. "Where's a town... Or someplace where we can get help?"

Chadwick grins at her, shakes his head and coughs out a spray of blood-tinged spittle. Pack looks concerned and nods his head toward a cluster of palm trees. "Here... Let's set him down in the shade."

The pilot's boot heels drag in the sand as they move him to a shady spot under the trees that provides a good view of the sailboat, open water, and blue-sky horizon beyond.

When they set him down, he gingerly leans back on a tree. Elliott gently removes the aviator's helmet and goggles, and then she smooths aside the sweat-matted hair on his forehead. "Will this be okay?"

Chadwick nods and calmly regards the small waves lapping on the sandy shore. "I want to show you something." He uses the pistol, which is still clenched in his bloody fingers, to gesture them both closer. He peers up at them and smiles. Turning to Elliott he says, "I bought something for you."

Pack and Elliott both lean in closer as the voice of the injured airman fades. Chadwick looks down at his wound and back up again. Abruptly, he drapes one arm around Elliott and the other, still brandishing the handgun, around Pack. Staring ahead, the pilot nods to the boat anchored offshore. "Sure is a beauty... Guess I won't be fit enough to enjoy it."

Glancing down to the mortal gunshot wound, Elliott notices that it is still seeping. She tries, unsuccessfully, to stop the flow by pressing the lapel of the pilot's coat against it. "Enjoy what?"

"There's where your money is at..."

Pack eyes the bloody, pistol-clenching hand resting over his shoulder and glances back to Chadwick. "It's on the boat?"

Chadwick sways his head to the side and chuckles softly. "They say money can't buy you freedom. Well, there it is…"

Pack slowly begins to understand the implication of Chadwick's statement, while Elliott stares blankly at the boat. She stands, letting Chadwick's limp arm drop to the sand as she steps toward the blue waters and looks out to the sailboat. In disbelief, she pivots and glares down at the dying airman. "You spent all the money on *that?!?*"

Slumping down as his life fades away, the flyer nods. "Couldn't think of a better way to go…"

Elliott stands staring at the sailing vessel and Pack climbs to his feet and joins her. "Elliott… You gonna be okay?"

She looks down to her feet, then up to her long-time partner and mutters in amazement, "He spent all that money on a boat…"

Chadwick lifts his head momentarily, puts on a smile, and then finally relaxes back against the trunk of a palm tree. "You know, ma'am, flyers and sailors have a lot in common… We both love the blue skies and the solitude of nature."

Standing side by side, Pack and Elliott gaze out past the gently rocking sailboat to the watery horizon. As if to convince them both of what's happened, she repeats again, "He spent all of the money..."

"Yeah."

"... On a boat."

A breeze turns the boat, pointing it out at sea, ready for its next adventure. Elliott contemplates a bit and then with renewed energy, turns to Pack. "Do you know how to sail?"

"Sure do."

Elliott makes peace with the situation and shrugs. "Alright, let's do it then." Stepping back toward Chadwick, she calls out "Let's go, fly-boy..."

Though the airman's eyes are open, there is no longer the animation of life in them. Elliott leans over and gently puts her hand upon his still chest. The tranquility of his once lively form suddenly overwhelms her with emotion. Pack kneels down beside them and places his hand over the pilot's eyes. Solemnly, he swipes them closed. Reflexively, the airman's eyes pop open wide again. Pack and Elliott exchange looks of surprise and then recheck him for any residual signs of life. After feeling for a pulse under the airman's chin, Pack shakes his head in disappointment. He gently lowers Chadwick's eyelids again, and they both take a reverent pause.

Closed for only a few seconds, the airman's eyelids pop open again. When Elliott gasps in astonishment, Pack offers, "I guess he's not ready yet."

Elliott takes her hand away from her mouth and nods. "We should give him another minute."

The two look at each other and then back to the body of the dead man lying between them. Pack nods his agreement. "It's kind of spooky."

"He was a little like that when he was alive, too."

They smile at another and then simultaneously turn to look out at the boat. Pack sighs, "He sure had good taste in sailing vessels, though…"

Contemplating the open waters ahead, Elliott moves away from the body on the beach. She unbuckles her cartridge belt and lets the holster and gun drop to the sand at her feet. Looking seductively over her shoulder, she smiles at Pack. "Won't be needing this…"

He watches as she walks toward the water, unties her neckerchief and lets it flutter to the ground.

He calls after her, "Where you going?"

She unbuttons her vest and lets it slip off her arms behind her, then leans down to grab at her feet to pull off her tall boots. "I'm going for a swim." Pack raises both eyebrows, as she unfastens her britches and lets them slide down her bare legs. Looking to the dead aviator, he places his open palm over the watching eyes. With only her shirt covering her, Elliott turns to Pack and waves him over. "Care to join me?"

Pack beams with excitement and starts to take off his boots. "Would love to...!" He pulls off his hat and bandana and lays them over Chadwick's face, before he trots across the beach while stripping away the rest of his clothing.

~*~

The wooden sailing vessel cuts through rolling waves under full sail. Pack sits bare-chested on the aft deck, rudder in hand, with his cowboy hat perched on the back of his head. He looks out to the open stretch of blue sea. He turns as Elliott, holding a set of copper mugs, comes up from the cabin below. "Ya find everythin' okay?"

Mexico Sky

She takes a sip from her cup and hands one to him. Raising her cup in a saluting gesture, she remarks. "He even stocked the galley." Elliott takes a seat by Pack at the helm, and nestles close. He puts his arm around her shoulder and gives a squeeze. "I guess you got everything you wanted?"

Elliott turns to Pack with a smoldering look while rubbing an open palm over her flat stomach. "Well... Just about."

As the sailing vessel cuts through the waves, with the sun high overhead, the shimmering water reflects rays of light up to the name on the boat. Written across the stern, in bold, freshly painted letters, it reads: *Mexico Sky*

The End.

If you enjoyed **Mexico Sky**, read other
stories by *Eric H. Heisner*

www.leandogproductions.com

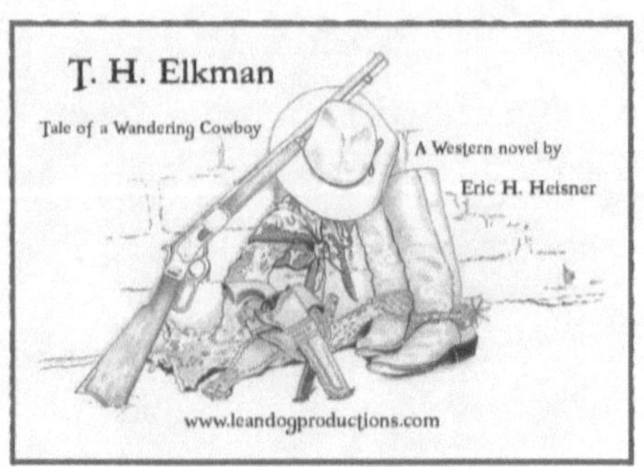
T. H. Elkman
Tale of a Wandering Cowboy
A Western novel by
Eric H. Heisner
www.leandogproductions.com

WEST TO BRAVO
A Western Novel
By Eric H. Heisner
WWW.LEANDOGPRODUCTIONS.COM

Wings of the Pirate
A high-flying Adventure Novel
By Eric H. Heisner
Limited time pre-order at:
www.inkshares.com
illustrations by
Al P. Bringas
www.leandogproductions.com

Eric H. Heisner is an award-winning writer, actor and filmmaker. He is the author of several Western and Adventure novels: *West to Bravo, Seven Fingers a' Brazos, T. H. Elkman, Along to Presidio,* and *Wings of the Pirate.* He can be contacted at his website: www.leandogproductions.com

Al P. Bringas is a cowboy artist, actor and horse lover. He has done illustrations for novels including: *West to Bravo, T. H. Elkman* and *Wings of the Pirate.* He lives and works in Pasadena, California.

www.ingramcontent.com/pod-product-compliance
Lightning Source LLC
Chambersburg PA
CBHW020755190726
48285CB00006B/2043